THE
MYSTERIES
OF
SOLDIERS
GROVE

PAUL ZIMMER

THE MYSTERIES OF SOLDIERS GROVE

THE PERMANENT PRESS
Sag Harbor, NY 11963

"Louise and Her Redoubtable Kingdom Come" appeared in a somewhat different format in the Gettysburg Review.

For information, address:
    The Permanent Press
    4170 Noyac Road
    Sag Harbor, NY 11963
    www.thepermanentpress.com

Library of Congress Cataloging-in-Publication Data

Zimmer, Paul.
    The mysteries of Soldiers Grove / Paul Zimmer.
        pages ; cm
    ISBN 978-1-57962-388-3 (hardcover)
        I. Title.

PS3576.I47M97 2015
813'.54—dc23   2014041249

Printed in the United States of America.

So that the retriving of these forgotten Things from Oblivion in some sort resembles the Art of a Conjuror, who makes those walke and appeare that have layen in their graves many hundreds of yeares: and to represent as it were to the eie, the places, Customes and Fashions, that were of old Times.

—John Aubrey's Brief Lives

CHAPTER 1

Cyril

I've given the slip to those officious people in the geezer home across the road, and tiptoed out the emergency exit when they thought I was taking a nap. It's late Friday afternoon in Soldiers Grove, the workweek is done, and Burkhum's Tap is filling up with thirsty, wiped-out people. I've staked myself out early at the bar, and dunked a few Leinenkugels already.

I've been trying to figure how I might tell a life or two to the guy sitting next to me, but I can see he's a weary man and I've learned to be cautious. Sometimes folks get the wrong idea when I start talking at them—like I am trying to put a move on them or something. So ridiculous! It makes me feel low when people misread me like that. It should be obvious to anyone that at my advanced age I couldn't even make an obscene phone call.

I've been a teller of lives and an odd jobs guy all my days, never having had the wit or strength to be a jock or cock or financial rock. Somehow I was lucky enough to discover that my only talent is for remembering the brief lives of famous people, and telling these little tales to other folks makes me feel useful, when I thought for a long time I had nothing to give.

But this is not easy work and lately I've been thinking about retirement. Some days I swear if I could locate the place in my brain where all these lives are assembled, I'd tilt my head to the side and drain them out through my ear hole into a bucket; then late one night I'd sneak out of the care home and go to the Soldiers Grove Public Library to funnel the whole thing into the book-drop slot. Our ingenious town librarian would find them in the morning on the floor in an iridescent puddle. This woman especially would know what to do with them. She'd carefully mop the lives up with a clean cloth and wring them into an elegant pitcher. Then, ding, ding, ding, she'd carefully pour them into one of the computers where they would mysteriously disperse, wash around and organize themselves with all the other information in those mysterious places so they can be instantly available to other people.

But then, after this, who would *tell* the lives? Who would give them the respect and care they need?

What would I do with myself? I'm still serving a purpose, and when I can't do this, I will be dead. Maybe I'll just keep them in my head. When I slip away finally—the whole load will just go out with me.

When I was a kid my parents were drunk and screaming at each other all the time. I can't remember what they said to each other but it was hateful and destructive. The slaughter went on endlessly through my childhood until one summer morning there was a miracle. A canny traveling encyclopedia salesman got his foot in our door when both my mother and father were home and only moderately clobbered. Quickly he sized up our situation. Burrowing into my parents' guilt, he convinced and shamed them into investing in the whole set of *Encyclopaedia Britannica* for their "smart little scholar" son.

When the huge load of boxes arrived a few weeks later we had no shelves to put the books on. My parents had forgotten they'd ordered them. So I had the deliveryman stack all the cartons to the left side of the front door. I opened the first box, took out volume one, went up to my room and began reading. Almost immediately I discovered that I liked the biographies best, so I concentrated on them. Devouring these lives, big and small, made the shrill sounds of my parents' combat fade away as I slowly worked my way through the accounts of famous folks in the big books.

When I became a teenager I saved money from grocery jobs and a paper route to buy my own set of the *Encyclopedia Americana* in installments. I had these boxes stacked on the right side of the front door as I acquired them, and devoured all the minibiographies in these imposing volumes until I'd finished high school.

The *Britannica* was my father, and the *Americana* was my mother—the only family I could count on. I also hung around the drugstore newsstand and scoured magazines, newspapers, and paperbacks for news of current luminaries. Sometimes I'd go to the bookstore in Viroqua or the Soldiers Grove library and hide in the biographical sections to peek in the books.

Without the brief lives I would have become some kind of scumbag. My folks spent all their time communing with spirits in bottles and there were no other more tangible apparitions in our house. I never met any grandparents, uncles, aunts, brothers, sisters, cousins, nephews, nieces—that sort of thing. There were a few tatty old photographs in drawers, but no identifying notes on the back.

I never knew why my parents hated each other so completely. Perhaps they felt trapped by my presence. That's a hell of a way to grow up. When they died, my father just weeks after my mother, I felt only numbness and shame that I had no tears, but I did not know how to feel sadness. Or perhaps I did not recognize the sadness that I felt. Or perhaps I had no sadness. I couldn't find an address book amongst their belongings, nor any real trace of an extended family in the miserable residue of the house, so I was the only person who attended their services.

After their deaths I thought about leaving Soldiers Grove, but did not know where to go, or how to go. I learned to drink beer (*no* spirits!) and over the years sometimes attended the local bars. I had a few occasional drinking buddies, but never figured out how to make close friends or talk to women.

While reading all those encyclopedia entries over the years, I put a lot of words into my vocabulary. Because of this some people think I talk funny and it makes them wary of me, but I keep chattering anyway. Sometimes I get a little pissed when I can't make them understand what I am talking about, but I try not to show this.

When I became elderly and finally couldn't manage for myself anymore, I took a room in the old folks' home. But I remain always hungry for *lives*: politicians, scientists, actors, musicians, scholars, soldiers, rogues, writers, artists, clergy, entertainers, criminals, architects, thinkers, athletes, and other famous people from the past. This is my real work. I want to know how these people got into and out of this world while doing something important enough to be meaningful. It is still my pleasure to collect this vicarious information and I try to share it with others.

❧

I'VE BEEN drinking beer at Burkhum's bar for at least half an hour, and now decided that I'm going to try and speak to the swarthy guy drinking next to me and give him one of my lives. I snap my fingers and cock my head at him.

"Got it!" I say.

He gives me a wary glimmer, and leans away as I tell him, "I've been trying to figure out who you remind me of. At first I was thinking Carmen Basilio, but then—maybe Vincente Minnelli or Camillo Benso, Count of Cavour? Then it hit me for sure—you are a dead ringer for Antonio Vivaldi."

It's just after five in the Tap and Burkhum's is starting to fill up now. According to our town sign posted on the highway, 593 people live in Soldiers Grove, so it is a quiet place. Occasionally over the years the town has been bedeviled by flooding problems, and about thirty years ago the business district and a lot of nice houses took a serious shot, swamped by spring overflowing. It had happened before, so the people decided to move the business section to higher ground and make part of the old residential section into a park. The little grocery, drug store, and farmers' hardware that were built on higher ground at that time all wasted away a decade or so ago, giving way to a Walmart Supercenter built in Viroqua, the larger market town twenty miles up the highway.

But still, in Soldiers Grove there's a Mobil station, a small motel/restaurant, a pharmacy, a very classy little library, post office, repair garage, Burkhum's Tap, and an American Legion Post with a World War II tank mounted in front, its cannon pointed across the highway at the nursing home where I live now.

I've grown old and require assisted living. I never knew how to have a girlfriend, never married nor had the courage to risk living with someone after witnessing the years of my parents' carnage. I just worked jobs in town and spent my spare time collecting brief lives. I know it's an odd calling. But this is what I've got.

The guy beside me in the Tap is wearing spattered bib overalls and a grimy Milwaukee Brewers cap. He's in the bar for a quick drink before heading home to his family and a washup after a hard week. He has puffy cheeks like Vivaldi's.

"You look Italian," I say to him. "Not too many Romans in Soldiers Grove." He won't look at me and doesn't chuckle at my little joke. I suppose he's heard of my reputation as a chatterbox.

But I am going to get something done. I've ducked out on those fussy folks in the nursing home, and now I'm on my fourth Leinenkugel. Every couple weeks or so I make a break for it and cut myself this slack. Otherwise I'd go bonkers, locked up with all those geriatrics. I've gone through three roommates, trying to tell them some of my lives. The last one attempted suicide, so now they've assigned me permanently to a private room.

I speak loudly to my neighbor in the Tap so he can hear me over the omnipresent television set mounted above the bar. Other patrons cast a wary eye at me.

"Antonio Vivaldi was a late seventeenth-century Italian composer, and lived halfway into the eighteenth," I say. The guy beside me is looking panicky, so I hurry on before he can bolt: "You may know his composition, *Four Seasons.* Probably you've heard it on an elevator in Madison or some-where—but Vivaldi composed a lot of other great stuff, too: concertos, a bunch of oratorios, more than ninety operas. He wrote pieces for lute and viola da gamba and pianoforte, cho-rales—even songs for solo voice. He made his living teaching music in a fancy school for orphan girls. He was an ordained priest, but he was always sniffing around the young ladies and sometimes the prefects had to send him away to cool off."

I give these little twists in my biographies sometimes to give them a snap that folks in Soldiers Grove might relate to.

"Oh . . . yeah?" the guy says to me out of the side of his mouth. He still hasn't looked at me.

"What's your name?" I ask. "Mine's Cyril." I stick my hand out for a shake.

He's slow to respond, but at last he says, "Vern," and holds out some limp fingers for me to grasp.

"Well, Vern, let me tell you a little more that might sur-prise you: Vivaldi apparently had some influence on Johann Sebastian Bach. They lived around the same time, and schol-ars have found transcriptions of Vivaldi's music in Bach's hand. They never met, but it seems like Bach might have taken some leads from Vivaldi. Bach wrote a lot of music, and he was a raunchy guy, too, but he wasn't hung up being a priest like Vivaldi, so he had twenty-two kids."

Vern finally gives me a quick flash, to make sure I don't seem too dangerous, then he swishes his drink around and drains it to the cubes. It looks like a double Jack Daniel's. That was my father's drink—starting around eight in the morning.

"Vivaldi was a grouchy guy, too," I hurry on, "he was always stewing about things. Maybe his chastity made him irritable. He used to pack a knife in his cloak, and if anyone messed with him on the street in Venice, he'd back them off fast." I'm pumping this part up too, trying to make things interesting for Vern, but I see he's trying to signal Burkhum for his tab.

"I got to go see to my milking," he explains from the side of his mouth.

I hurry on, "One time Vivaldi sliced up a gondolier for shortchanging him, but they let him off without a charge because he was in the middle of composing an oratorio for the king. In those days governments gave you a little credit for being artistic."

Burkhum comes over—but before Vern can ask for his bill, I say, "Hey, Burkhum, give me another Leinie, and I'd like to buy Vern here another of whatever he's drinking." Vern relaxes just a little now. Double mixed drinks cost four big ones in the Tap, and Burkhum puts out big plastic bowls of fresh popcorn on Friday nights.

"Maybe you don't favor music, Vern," I say. "I see you're wearing a Brewers hat. How about a little baseball? You know you look a little like Cookie Lavagetto, too." Vern is starting to look uneasy again. Burkhum brings our drinks and Vern takes a big pull on his double, but doesn't thank me. I go on talking.

"Cookie came up with the Pirates in 1934, and then was traded to Brooklyn in '37. He became the Dodgers' regular third baseman in '39 and hit .300. But in a few years he got drafted for the war and didn't get back to baseball until '46. Mostly he warmed the bench for the Dodgers then because they had Spider Jorgensen playing third. In the '47 World

Series against the Yankees, in the fourth game, Bill Bevens is tossing a no-hitter in the ninth, but he walks the first two guys. The Dodgers decide to put Cookie in to pinch hit, and he smacks a double off the right field wall to ruin Bevens's no-hitter and beat the Yankees 2-1. Cookie is king of Brooklyn.

"How did the Dodgers thank Lavagetto for this? They released him the next season. He'd given them everything he had. Baseball's like Russian communism. You get the red star one day, and you disappear the next."

Vern seems a little more interested in this biography, but he is still leaning away like he's expecting me to explode at any minute.

"Hey, Vern," I say. "Am I boring you? That's all I know about Cookie Lavagetto and Antonio Vivaldi. Would you like to know what I know about Alfred Sisley or Buck Clayton? Harold Stassen? Cagliostro? Bucky Pizzarelli? Sara Teasdale? Saint James the Greater? Amelita Galli-Curci? How about Sonny Tufts? Sister Kenny? Maybe you like those Italians. Cosimo de Medici? Boom Boom Mancini? Johnny Antonelli? Amedeo Modigliani?"

But Vern is gone. He knocks his glass over making his break and spills ice cubes down the bar. Everyone's looking at me, and I feel like a backhoe on a wet clay tennis court. What the hell *is* wrong with me? Why do I go on gassing like this? Why can't I just stay in my room and keep my trap shut?

Because I have all this stuff in my head—I've got to let some of it out once in a while or I'll explode. I mean, what the hell! I am keeper of the *lives*! That's important. This is my work, but I'm like a guy who mucks out barns for a living. People stand clear of me.

Burkhum brings me the bill. "Bring me another Leinie, please," I say.

"That's enough today, Cyril," Burkhum says. "The nurses are going to be in here looking for you in a minute, and they're going to give me holy hell as it is."

"Well, I don't want to be a problem for you." I pay my tab. "Say, Burkhum, did anyone ever tell you, you look like Sinclair Lewis?" Burkhum quick steps away.

Just as I'm fixing to put on my stocking cap and leave the Tap, a guy I know from the nursing home comes in the door. His name is Nobleson. He lives in the "self-sufficient" section and can take a powder anytime he wants. He doesn't have to sneak out like I do. Nobleson checks out the crowd and sees me waving to him. He hesitates, but then slowly heads over because he knows I've got dough and will buy him a drink.

"Nobleson," I greet him. "How're you, buddy boy? Sit down here for a minute. What are you drinking? You know, when you were walking over here I was thinking to myself that you look like Arthur Godfrey."

Nobleson knows the course, so he steers me in a direction he favors more. "Not me," he says. "You're thinking about somebody else. But I've always been told that I look a lot like a young Van Johnson."

"Now *there's* a guy!" I say to Nobleson.

Burkhum has approached us. "Double Old Crow on ice," Nobleson tells him.

"And give me another Leinie," I say.

"Crow coming up," says Burkhum, "but no Leinie for you, Cyril. You need a nap."

Burkhum is sometimes an obscenity. "Burkhum," I say to him, "you remind me of George Jeffreys. You know who he was?"

Burkhum wipes off the bar in front of us, but he doesn't answer.

"He was the hanging judge for King James; the 'Bloody Assizer,' they called him, the keeper of the seal. The king's muscle. He'd swing anyone from the gallows if they mouthed off about the king. No questions asked—and no defense allowed."

"Sure, Cyril," Burkhum says. "And I'll be a bloody abettor if I give you another Leinie." Burkhum might be a prick, but

I have to admit, he has some snap. He went to the university in Madison for a year before he started tending bar.

"But you!" I turn back to Nobleson, "You *are* a ringer for a young Van Johnson."

I have to admit here, I'm in a bit of a panic, scuffling with my gray cells, trying to come up with the goods on Johnson. I'm getting just a little rusty as I get older. I haven't thought about Van Johnson in years, and the four Leinies have addled me a bit—but there's some Johnson stuff in there, I know it, and I can feel it beginning to shake loose, the filamentous branching of my neurons is extending. Then—aha! Bingo.

"*The Human Comedy,* now wasn't Van Johnson in that? He played a young guy going off to the Second World War. Wasn't that his first movie?" Clickety-click-click, I was on my way now. "Mickey Rooney was in it, too. And Frank Morgan. From a William Saroyan novel. Schmaltzy, but pretty good. It was okay to be a little sappy in those days.

"Let's see. What was next for Van Johnson? *A Guy Named Joe*. Then *Thirty Seconds Over Tokyo*. They liked him playing young soldiers. Hell of a story. Pilot gets shot down and loses his B-25. Johnson did a heap of suffering in that movie. That was a big one for him. You're right, buddy. You *do* look like him. He was a pretty boy."

Nobleson is smiling at me in a sort of wonder. "You are a living Google," he says, and shakes his head.

I'm not sure I know what he means, but I don't think it's an insult—something about all this electric gibberish floating through the air these days—but I was buttering him up, trying to keep him sitting on his stool. "Van Johnson . . . let's see. *The Last Time I Saw Paris*, with Elizabeth Taylor. He was a soldier in that one, too. Wow! Can you imagine? Johnson was 4-F in Hollywood during the war. All the other guys were off fighting. All those lonely actresses. I'll bet he used to get more ass than a toilet seat when he was making it big. But then some folks claimed he was gay, so maybe he was even working both sides of the pump."

Oh-oh! Too much. I'd gotten overly excited. I talked too loud and everyone in the bar heard that scatology. I put that last bit in just to give the story some zing. Sometimes the lives need a little pepping up, you know—but now I'm over the top. I try to hurry on with something else. "Johnson was born in Rhode Island," I say. I think that's actually true. I pulled that out of my ratty hat—pretty damned good for an assisted-living guy.

But too late—Burkhum is standing in front of me, and he is not impressed. He doesn't allow dirty talk in his bar. "Cyril, there's ladies in here. You're getting kind of salty. You need to go outside and breathe some cold air."

Nobleson has drained his glass and is gone. I pay the tab, pull on my stocking cap, slip into my coat, and shuffle out the door into the winter.

Hard snow is flying sideways, but I don't want to go back to that pissified room in assisted living just yet. I pull my collar up, duck my head, and walk across the parking lot to the Mobil station.

A guy's pumping some lead free into his pickup, so I walk over to him and ask, "How you doin'?" The man has his head covered in one of those button-down fur balaclavas, so I can't see his face.

"You got any money?" That's all he says. His voice is sort of croaky, coming out of that big hat. I don't answer his question, so when the gas pump snaps off, he shoves the nozzle back in the cradle, claps his arms around his sides to warm himself up, and hustles into his truck to get out of the cold. But he cranks his window partway down. "I mean it, brother," he says. "I could use a little help."

His covered face makes him mysterious, but I try to size him up so I can give him a life. I say, "You know, with that hat on, you look like Elisha Kent Kane." I step up to his window so he can hear me over the wind. "You probably don't know who Kane was. He was a doctor from Philly and one of the earliest arctic explorers. He got his party lost in the tundra in 1855, but he led them on a hike all the way out to Greenland. It took three months, and they damned near all froze to death, but he kept them plugging along and saved most of them in the end. They put his picture on a postage stamp, and there were parades and national celebrations, but you don't hear much about Elisha Kent Kane anymore."

The wind boots up through the gas pumps and a tin "Self Service" sign is swinging and squawking just over my head. "She's fixing to snow good," I say. I'd forgotten my big scarf in Burkhum's and was starting to feel the cold.

"How about it, grandpa, you going to give me a hand with my gas?" the guy asks again. The gas pump is ringing and buzzing now. The guy's tone is tetchy and uneven. "I'm running short. Got to make it all the way to Peoria tonight."

"They're talking more than a foot of snow on the radio," I say. I'm beginning to feel a little uneasy. The guy seems weird. But I still can't help myself: "That reminds me. There was this guy named Snow—C.P. Snow—in the fifties and sixties, a scientist who started writing novels as a hobby, and got deep into it. One of those real smart Brits. They made him a peer, and he was always trying to mix literary stuff with scientific in his novels. It started out as a good shtick for a while and he cleaned up with some best sellers. Lord Snow. Not many folks read him these days."

I can't see the balaclava guy's eyes, but I feel his mean look from deep in the fur. I know he's wondering which wall I'd bounced off of. That's the way it is with me.

"What the fuck are you talking about?" he growls from deep in his cold throat.

"Well, good luck on Peoria," I say, and make to head off. "I better get back to my room."

"Hold it, pops!" His voice snaps off and shatters on me like icicles from a spouting. "Get in." He's lowered his window all the way and has something pointed at me. It is one *hell* of a gun he is holding, more like some sort of monstrous pipe fitting.

"I'm just an old man," I say. "I don't have anything that would help you."

"Get your creaky ass into the truck!"

I make another move to walk away, but he shouts, "*Now*, geezer—or you die!"

I know he means it. I hobble around to the other side of his truck, pull the door handle, and struggle in. "I don't know what you want, but folks are going to be looking for me," I say.

He turns on his ignition and hits the gas pedal all in one motion, and his truck jumps forward. Somebody in the station flashes lights, but he doesn't stop; he's down the drive, spinning fast without looking onto the highway. Snow is really flying now and beginning to mount. There must be four inches down already. He hasn't paid for his gas, and he's making fast on the icy road out of Soldiers Grove with me in his passenger seat. He's a mean guy, and I'm thinking that all the lives in the world aren't going to save my ass now.

Heavy snowflakes twist down into the windshield. We are barreling toward Readstown through windblown drifts. "You can have all the money in my wallet," I say. "There must be about twenty-five in there." He doesn't answer.

"You know, Clifford Brown was killed in snow like this," I tell him. "He was a great jazz trumpeter, made all kinds of innovations. He was helping some motorist who got stuck in a drift, and another car going too fast started sliding and wasted him."

Jazz. That was the music I listened to when I was young— even now. I have stacks of 78s, 45s, tapes and CDs going way back. I always favored the music, felt like it saved my life sometimes because it was great enough to blow my blues away.

But I don't think it's going to save my life now. Nothing is. This guy doesn't listen to any jazz. I can tell. He doesn't listen to anything. He unloosens his balaclava and folds the flaps back from over his mouth. He's got a greasy black beard, and a mouth like an open cut. "Why don't you shut your fuckin' trap?" he says. I can tell he's a man who doesn't care where he goes or what he does, so long as he's getting away. He's not even going to Peoria. But he's got me in his truck now.

There are no other cars on the road. Decent, sensible folks stay home on nights like this. You can't even see the lights of Readstown through the blizzard. For a moment the truck starts wavering and sliding almost sideways, but he takes his foot off the gas, manages to straighten the vehicle out of its slide, and slows down only a little. You can tell he's driven desperately in snow before. He doesn't care.

I've got to do something—so I start talking again, "One time Jesse James and his brother, Frank, were up north raising hell in Minnesota." The guy twists in his seat and I don't know if he's going to hit me or shoot me. To make things worse, now my groin is aching. I forgot to use the men's room in Burkhum's before I left. I have to pee. I mean I *really* have to pee.

But I keep talking. "Jesse and Frank are taking what they can get. They go into the bank in a little town, pull guns, and line all the people up against a wall. Some women have fainted and little kids are crying. The bank clerk is moving too slow and Jesse knows he is stalling, so he tells Frank to shoot the guy in the foot just to show they mean business. Frank blows off the guy's big toe right through his shoe. He's howling on the floor, but Jessie and Frank haul him up bleeding and make him open the safe."

I can tell in the darkness that the balaclava guy is listening. It's his kind of story. So I start to give it a little twist.

"There's an old man amongst the hostages, and he's not in good shape. He's gasping and clutching his chest like he's going to drop from a heart attack. Jesse sees this and he feels bad. He's partial to old guys because his father'd been good to him when he was a boy."

This is whole cloth, I admit—but I am out here zipping through cold darkness with this balaclava guy and his monster gun, and I'm spinning a story as fast as I can think it up. Maybe it will help me.

"Jesse has some mercy," I go on. "He takes the old guy by his arm and helps him to the door and—to the amazement of the people in the bank—he lets him go. Then the James boys make about finishing their business, scooping up bloody bundles of cash and running for their horses. But some of those town folks in the bank were cheering Jesse and Frank as they rode away."

This last is too much of a spin. "Get off it, you old shit-head!" Balaclava snarls.

"I've got to pee," I say.

"What are you sayin' to me? Tough shit!"

"I'm going to do it in my pants!" I warn urgently.

"Not my problem."

"It'll get all over your upholstery."

We haven't passed another car yet, and Balaclava is whizzing down the middle of the road. "We're the only two people in the whole county crazy enough to be out on a night like tonight," I say. "Except the sheriff. I know him. He'll be out watching for anyone speeding in this weather. By now he knows somebody's skipped paying at the Mobil."

Balaclava thinks about this for a minute, and looks into his rearview mirror. Then he says, "Bite it off, old man!" He still has his huge gun on his lap.

"I've got to pee!" I try to keep quiet, but I feel it beginning to seep into my long johns.

"What is this? Grade school?" Balaclava is really irritated.

"If you shoot me, I'll just bleed all over your upholstery, too."

Balaclava abruptly starts pumping his brakes and the car is slowing down, wavering and slipping as he eases it toward the side of the highway almost sliding off into the berm.

Cyril, I say to myself, *this is it. Now you've done it. You've recited your last brief life.* But I give it one last best shot—I say to Balaclava as the storm batters around us, "You remember Neil Armstrong, the first moon walker? He was born in a little town in Ohio, and they made him commander of the first moon mission, even though he was a civilian. It was 1969. When he stepped out of the Apollo onto the moon he said some famous stuff about taking one small step for man, a giant leap for mankind, but when he wrote a book about it later, he claimed he was really thinking—just at that very moment when he first put his foot down in the white moon dust—about his old father in a care home back in Ohio. He was recalling how the old man was always gentle to everyone and everything. He wanted to remember this so that if he came across any moon creatures, he'd know to be kind to them."

This was the most whole cloth I'd ever spun. It didn't matter. "Jesus Christ, old man!" Balaclava snaps. "*You* are from the moon." I thought he was going to laugh, but he says, "How do you shovel anything that deep?" He picks up his considerable gun and points it at me.

I'm thinking that I'm done.

"Give me your fucking wallet and get out of my truck before you start pissing on my seat."

I fall to my hands and knees in the snow when I get out of his truck. Balaclava doesn't shoot me. I struggle up and watch his taillights disappear in the swirl. The snow is driving hard and horizontal, and the wind is slicing. I pull my stocking cap way down to my eyes and over my ears. The frigid whiteness is up to my calves and over my boot tops. It is coming into my wrists between my sleeves and gloves. It's ten miles between Soldiers Grove and Readstown and I figure I'm about halfway. Out here the farms are so far in off the road you can't even see their lights.

My wet underpants and long johns start freezing to my groin, my scarf is back on a stool in Burkhum's Tap, so the wind runs its cold fingers down my neck. Cyril, I say to myself, get your butt moving. It's only five miles. I start shuffling back in the direction of Soldiers Grove, toward my warm, little room in the home.

Who do I start with? George Mikan? Heinrich Kühn? The Empress Marie Louise? Bingo Binks? Catherine of Valois? Ji Chang? Siegfried Sassoon? Dodo Marmarosa, General Alexis Kaledin? Nelly Sachs? Gorgeous George? Ségolène Royal? Thomas à Kempis? Colley Cibber? Suetonius? Édouard Vuillard? Heinrich Heine? Barbara Jordan?

Elisha Kent Kane! The guy who walked out of the snow. That's it. That's the guy. Cyril, you're on your way to Greenland. It's going to take awhile.

Chapter 2

Louise

This late-autumn chill—what happened to summer? I remember only shuffling through dog-day heat in a stupor, through hallways from one clinic to another, sitting by a window in my house sweating with a lap rug over my aching knees in August, watching a neighbor take hay from our fields. I recall ingesting many medicines, falling down on several occasions, and after a spell on the floor alone, struggling up alone to tend my bruises. That was summer.

When neighbors express concern I say, "Oh, I'm all right, I'm just taking my turn," and put on a plucky smile. I've worn many masks in my life, absorbed many blows and finally, losing Heath, my husband, knocked me permanently askew. Now growing old is a final cudgeling. At times I feel resentful about this last tussle, but then I suppose everyone feels a bit cheated when the end comes into sight.

Just awake from a nap and feeling chilled from the snowy weather outside, I snug my shawl around my shoulders. Firewood is stacked outside the door in the hutch Heath made for us, but I am not yet sufficiently confident of my strength to struggle up and make it to the door to bring in an armful.

❧

HEATH. I think of the first time I saw him in his American army uniform more than sixty years ago, bright as a yearling deer, believing he could do everything. He'd won my attention, then my heart—and that was not an easy thing to do. Many had tried to turn my head, but I'd been the star student at the *académie* and had my mind set on other things besides men.

The world war fighting had swept back and forth through our village three times and, in its course, destroyed half my family—I'd lost my father and a sister. It didn't seem that grief would ever end. But France was recovering now, things were going uphill again, and I had things to do. I was young, ambitious, and poised to rise above my losses—like young Heath, I assumed I was deathless and that all things were possible. I wanted to paint, write poems, play the piano, study in Paris, meet artists and interesting people, find my own essence, and try new things. I was ready to *live* my life.

But Heath, the stunning liberator, the wholehearted, blond American, surprised me—he would become so buoyant when he described the beauty of his Wisconsin farm to me, making it sound like a verdant park. "How couldn't we be happy together in those driftless hills? The two of us," he would ask as he held me close. "We must marry and you will come with me. We'll be like Adam and Eve in the garden," he said.

My mother, who called Heath *le garçon d'or*, the golden boy, was torn—not certain at all that she wanted to have her only remaining daughter marry and go away to America. But Heath was quite a *prix*. My mother had been permanently shaken by the war and loss of her husband and a daughter. There was little left of what we owned and loved. She wanted good things for her remaining child. America was good. The war had not touched there. Money and power were there.

My mother had many brothers and an unmarried sister she could live with in France to help stave off her loneliness. We talked and talked; some days she urged me to go with Heath, other days she threatened to lock me in my room. But travel was cheap after the war. We decided that, if I went with Heath, I could come home to France often for visits. Perhaps my mother could even come to America for stays. We would write often to each other. Heath was a "man of property," he was engaging, he was strong and beautiful, he had a clear mind, he was in love with me, wanted to marry me, he seemed a gentle person—and he was an American.

With young Heath holding me in his strong arms, I began to believe that perhaps I *could* do the things I wanted to do in the beautiful countryside of Wisconsin. I became so confused and overwhelmed by his enthusiasm and declarations of love that sometimes I would suddenly turn and flee from him. Heath had the good sense not to pursue me when I did this. He knew enough to give me some space and time.

When I saw him again vigorously striding down the street toward me, I'd think to run away from him once more, so not to be confused. But I did not run. Heath would be smiling, full of enthusiasm and more ideas—and when he talked and looked off into the distance, his eyes were Scandinavian blue like I imagined Wisconsin skies must be.

We tried to make plans. When he described his farm and drew some maps, it seemed possible to me that together we could make the place into a sort of park. We would border our acres of grass and grain with beds of flowers. I would create sculptures to place on the lawns. There would be green, well-tended paths through our woodlands. We would have many children to frolic on our lawns. I imagined we would host *soirees* for rustic artists and writers. Heath would buy me a piano, and our family would sing together—Berlioz and Gershwin songs—we would tell stories together and gaze out at the grandeur of the seasons on our small estate.

❧

As I look out now across the fields toward our woods I see the first challenge of the impending winter, snowflakes flurrying, skittering just outside my window on the deck that Heath had built many years ago. Still I do not feel strong enough to rise from my chair and bring in some firewood.

My cassette player is on the table beside my chair. I select a tape and snap it into the machine. If I do not yet have strength to build fire, I can at least have music. I think about putting on some jazz—Duke Ellington, Lester Young? Perhaps something quiet and contemplative like Oscar Peterson or Miles Davis. But instead, in the chill, I select a warm classic—Villa-Lobos, the fourth Bachianas Brasileiras, played by Alma Petchersky, which I'd ordered recently from the Musical Heritage Society. I turn my hearing aids up and close my eyes. Villa-Lobos's rich, repeating tropical theme would have pleased Bach, I like to imagine, the music crossing and swooping over itself like flocks of jungle birds in the sun. After a while I dip into slumber, and the music engages my dreams. The rain forest becomes an orchestra and Heath and I are dancing in a green *salle de bal*. Somewhere a phone is ringing.

I awaken distressed. How long had the phone been ringing? Someone from the care home seeking my answer? The phone is silent now. It is cold in the living room, and snow is mounting beyond the deck in the yard outside my window and in the fields and bare branches of the trees. Beyond this I see it is sweeping out to the valley and beginning to cover the driftless hills.

At last I set the lap rug aside and painfully push myself up from the chair, tighten my shawl around my shoulders, shuffle across the room, open the door and step out to the firewood stacked just outside the door. The sudden cold makes me feel dizzy as snow swirls around the house, but I manage to gather up an armful of wood, enough to start warming up the living room. I bring it in to the fireplace, lay the fire with some tinder, and strike a kitchen match. Just the sight of small flames catching and spreading makes me feel stronger.

In a while I will bring in more wood and prepare a bit of supper for myself. It will be a simple meal—perhaps a cut-up apple and a bowl of soup heated from the tureen brought over by a thoughtful neighbor. But I will rest some more before I do this task.

A week ago someone called from the senior home in Soldiers Grove to say there is a room available. I must do something, make a decision soon.

I fear acquiescence and change. This hilltop has become my world. It began as my home away from home, but now it is part of my spirit. How can I leave this place that I have arduously grown to love—this solitude that I in time was able to accept and cherish?

If I leave, where will the music go? Where will I keep my books? Where will I write poems? Where will I paint? Where will the still days of silence go, the mysterious sounds of weather and the seasons, and my own voice talking to itself? This air that is so fresh, where will it go? The birds swooping onto my feeders, and the great trees that I once walked to for visits every day on paths that strung through distant woods that spread now only in my mind as I sit in my chair. Where will they go?

The farm has been closing in around me, the woodland is unkempt and its paths overgrown. The cows have been sold. The fields are untidy, cut hastily by a worker from a co-op farm that rents them. I pay a young man to mow the grass close to my house, but the extended lawns that Heath and I created are wild now with hardscrabble weeds, and my sculptures are swarmed over with vines and prickly ash.

But to give all this up for an air-conditioned, sepulchral room in a building crowded with other elders? There seems to be no decision here, and yet there is a decision that must be made. I have never been brave, yet I was plucky enough to come to these hills years ago—it does not matter now whether I was right or wrong, it is time to reach again into my meager reserve of courage.

⤬

I⊤ WASN'T that Heath changed when we first arrived at the farm in Wisconsin, but his focus was redirected. He was once again locked back into routine and custom. I realized quickly that he had no choice—his instincts were overwhelming. His older brother had been caretaking the farm while Heath was in the service and had done his best—but now it was time for Heath to take up the ceaseless work: moving our cows from pasture to pasture, mending fences, cleaning our barns, cultivating and planting hay, mowing, raking, baling the cuttings, milking the cows. He had no choice. The work enveloped him from dawn to dusk.

Heath took such care in tending our fields. As I watched him he was like a poet masterfully cutting his rows of grass—windrowing them as if he were polishing his lines. Then his machine swallowed the rows of hay, and rolled out bales like poems—and the land was cleared again for a short while like a blank page.

In summer I would carry our lunches out to the acres in a basket and join him to sit under a large, solitary oak that had been left standing in the middle of the fields. Heath would be sodden with sweat, seeds and broken stems in his eyebrows and blond beard, but he would gather his energy to chat with me as we rested. In winter I would go and seek him in the barns as he worked with our cows, but sometimes he was so busy and preoccupied he could only speak briefly, his mind and body overwhelmed by duties and chores.

Soon after we came to the farm I recognized that this was what he had been born to. Had he conveniently forgotten these responsibilities when he held me in his arms in France? Had he effaced this from his mind when we were so young? Had he misrepresented? I do not hold any of this against

Heath. He loved me, wanted me to come to America with him. That seemed to be all that was on his mind at that time. He was a guileless man, at all times grateful for my presence. I never asked him if he had forgotten.

In the evenings after supper we would retire together to our living room to read, and I would put on some music; Heath would turn the pages of one of his agricultural magazines as I read my books. He tried hard, but before long, in his weariness, he would nod off. I would gently shake him; we checked the windows, turned out the lights and went to our bed.

During our first years together I had two dangerous, almost fatal miscarriages which—in our remote rural environment, many miles from medical care—were such very close calls, frightening us into deciding against further attempts to have children. This was a fact, like many others, that I learned to live with.

Heath and I rarely had time to take walks together, but every day I strolled the ridges of our woods alone, over the weatherworn driftless hills, which had been gently shaped over the eons by the elements and not gouged out by glaciers. I fancied these serene rises in summer, the patient competition of their vegetation, their flush, slow-motion scrambling, feeling the comfort of the cool rustle of trees as I strolled in the green light beneath their canopies. I cherished them in all seasons, their changes, colors, the winds battering, and their snow-laden branches above the deep drifts when the blowing stilled.

I loved the edges of our woods as well, the in-between places where mowers could not reach, so fraught with changing growth and wildflowers, such delicacy through this fervent striving, sometimes the tiniest blossoms appearing on uplifted chandeliers of green stems, or the sudden, petite flowers that lasted only a day or two like reminders of forgotten times, or the weeds that split and spread across each other in intricate green patterns.

But my favorite time in the woods was late autumn, when I could go out by myself in jacket and gloves to shuffle through thick drifts of leaves to look far down our ridge through naked stands.

Many things are revealed about trees when just a few scattered rags of yellow leaves are wagging on their branches. The limbs and crisscrossing trunks record the achievements of summer. Their bare abundance gave me comfort. I could count on their verdure to return after the coming snow and cold.

Then the snow. After the first tentative sprinkles, it would one day rush in to blanch and overwhelm the hills and valleys in sculptured whiteness for months on end, giving face to the winds.

And so the driftless hills were my Eden, in their varied attitudes, my redoubtable kingdom come. This is the place that Heath brought me to so many years ago.

Late in our marriage, one spring day there was a sudden, hard afternoon rain, which passed quickly and gave way to sunshine again. Heath, spreading manure in the fields, had been soaked. When he came in that evening, he stopped outside the screen door to take off his reeking work boots.

When he came in he looked so weary and soiled with his work, smelling like an animal himself, almost embarrassed to be in the kitchen; I went to hug him but he gently held me off and grasped me at arm's length before bending forward to kiss my forehead. He was shamed to be so soiled. I wrung my apron—then hastened to lift the teakettle as it began to shriek on the stove.

Heath reached around and slipped something from his back pocket. It was a surprise. I don't know what had prompted him—he'd never before done such a thing—but on his way in from the fields he'd paused to pick a spray of wildflowers for me and wrapped it in a large tree leaf. As he placed the bouquet in my hand he was damp with grime and the whiff of dung. He had arranged the flowers carefully with even some sprigs of green intermingled.

He seemed to be amazed himself by what he'd done—the flowers were such tender, intricate things in his rough, unwashed hand.

My own surprise preempted speech, but I removed one yellow blossom, went to Heath and slipped its stem into the top buttonhole of his soiled work shirt. Before our eyes could meet, I moved to the cupboard to find a Mason jar for the bouquet, filling it halfway with water from our tap. The flowers fanned out gratefully as I placed them in the water. I went to Heath again and leaned to kiss his weathered cheek.

Heath opened large gardens for me when we arrived on the farm, and at first I grew flowers, but over time these gave way to the vegetables we needed. If Heath and I walked together, we walked on Sundays. Then we worked at keeping our paths clear through the woods. When we talked together, usually it was in the evenings after supper, about fertilizer or rainfall or the cost of seed brands. In the early mornings before he left for his work we chatted over coffee about local things, neighbor gossip, dog stories, house problems. Then he would be gone to the fields.

I assisted Heath as much as I could with the farming. I tended small animals, grew the garden, kept the accounts, made our reports to the natural resources department, did the shopping, and ran errands to town. I was not able to work for long hours out of doors in the high heat of growing season, so I stayed in the house, reading and listening to music during those days, and this helped to sustain me while Heath labored in the fields. Occasionally I attempted a watercolor or worked at sculptures that I constructed from baling wire, old bolts and broken parts of farm equipment. I worked at my journal and poems. I practiced at our upright piano and over the years taught myself six Chopin nocturnes. On occasion I would play one of them for Heath as he sat so weary in his chair at the end of the day, and he seemed genuinely proud of me, sweetly applauding when I finished.

I had supper ready on time and Heath was always grateful for whatever I cooked for him; but early in our life together I perceived something—he was uncomplaining, but I could see that he did not favor French cuisine. So I prepared potatoes, soft vegetables and red meat for him, which he ate hungrily in his weariness.

Our life together was not as I had imagined it—but I allowed myself no lingering bitterness. I had no right to feel cheated. Heath had not lied to me. I had romanced and misperceived—had allowed myself to misjudge things, had manufactured my own dreams. We *were* Adam and Eve—but the serpent had come and gone. And I was far from home.

Heath had no choice but to do the work. I had nowhere to go beyond the farm, no one to talk to, nothing to do but cook, clean, read books, listen to music, work occasionally at my art, and tend the garden. Our rural neighbors—warm-hearted, generous people—do not speak of Mallarmé, de Beauvoir, Poulenc or Vuillard. Western Wisconsin Technical College is not the Sorbonne. I learned to be alone.

But how could I begrudge or be angry with Heath, who had stayed beautiful, loving, and true to his end—when he died of a farm accident, his tractor tipping over on him as he wearily turned a row at the edge of a rain-logged field. He'd grown less careful and alert about such things as he aged and his energies lessened. I found him crushed and bled to death in the weeds. It was the day of our wedding anniversary and we had planned to celebrate that evening with a sirloin dinner at the Driftless Tavern. I will not recover from the horror of his death. Ours was a quiet, misconceived life—but there was love, we did our work, endured and remained devoted.

I regret that I always must have seemed a tinge sad to him, but he grew to accept this as my nature.

❧

THE HEAD nurse from the care home called again to press me for a decision, and I have agreed to take their room. She visited my house with several assistants to have me sign papers. These women, I realized, were also taking stock of me. They were overly cheerful and laughed a great deal, but seemed puzzled, almost mildly threatened, by my houseful of books, recordings, and pictures. We sat in my living room and I gave them coffee. They admired the view from my windows.

I do not know what they concluded from their visit, but I felt myself being discussed as their car disappeared down my road. We made arrangements for their van to pick me up with a small load of my possessions, and they gave me an imposing pamphlet of rules and regulations with a color picture on the cover of relentlessly happy-looking elders opening gift packages.

I read everything carefully. There are a number of rules, some of them daunting, many of them threatening and cold. For instance, rule sixteen reads: "More than three (3) emergency calls in one month from an apartment to the switchboard shall be conclusive evidence to landlord that occupant is not capable of independent living. Landlord can then have tenant moved to such health care facility as available."

Chapter 3

Cyril

The sheriff and his deputy told me I looked like a quarter pickup load of grape popsicles when they found me on the road. They'd been looking for Balaclava after he jumped paying for his gas at the Mobil, and the station attendant had told them that he was pretty sure someone might have been abducted into the thief's car before it went flying off into the blizzard.

So the officers put on their blinker lights and were sweeping with their overhead spots along the drifted berm when they saw a mound of snow. That was me. Luckily they found me before the snowplows started coming through or I would have been chop suey.

I'd actually made it back to within a couple miles of Soldiers Grove before I was not able to move anymore. The storm was still gnashing over the landscape and my legs finally played out. My brain was slipping away, and my gonads were freezing so that at the end I was waddling like a duck right out of a winter lake. Finally I went down face first in the snow. I still had enough sense to realize—this is it, Cyril, you are ready for the long nap.

I was so immobilized, aching with cold, it didn't matter anymore. Bring it on! There are worse ways to go. You know the first thing I thought when I went down on the ground and felt the cold closing in toward my heart? Not about my miserable parents, nor my bar acquaintances in Soldiers Grove—and I was definitely not pleading to some preoccupied god and his angels. I was thinking about a life, about Captain Robert F. Scott and how he'd died trying to make it back from Antarctica. I was feeling probably like he must have felt on his last day—his bloodstream slowing down and his brain cells turning to frozen yogurt. He'd lost the race to the Antarctic Circle to Roald Amundsen, the Norwegian, and now he was going to lose his life, freezing to death in his tent. The final thing he wrote above his signature in his journal was, "It seems a pity, but I do not think I can write more—R. Scott."

It seemed a pity to me, too, that my life was going down in the below-zero drifts.

But the sheriff and his deputy swept the snow off me, hauled me stiff as a frozen lamb chop to their cruiser, and turned their heater up high. The sheriff drove as fast as he could on tire chains to the emergency room in Viroqua, while the deputy cuffed and slapped my cheeks, rubbed my hands, and thumped my chest in the backseat.

When they finally got me onto a cot in the ER my temperature was down in the eighties. I was ready to sign off, but I found out later that they covered me with some gizmo called a Bair Hugger—a big paper and plastic blanket with a hole in it. They fastened a tube into the hole and blew in warm air so that it hugged my body. They also strung me up with IVs of fluid, and gave me a warm enema. I think they did other things, too, to raise my temperature, but I can't say for sure because I was way out there ice skating on a chilled dream, like Ted Williams in his frozen time capsule—but I'd never won any batting championships in my day.

When I finally woke up into the half light of intensive care, I felt like I'd been cut open, had all my bones pulled out, and had them placed in a dirty bag—where the docs cracked them with a hammer, and then stuffed them back into my body.

It wasn't just *pain* I felt—but lonesomeness that washed over my spirit. I knew this empty drill from my childhood, but now I was into the big time. I was doing this all alone and there didn't seem to be anyone else in the whole expanding universe—just me, those wires and cords poked down my throat, and all those goddamned blinking little lights.

When finally they pulled the tubes out of my throat days later, nurses brought me warm drinks and pills to swallow. They listened to my heart all the time, every thirty seconds, it seemed to me. They checked my IVs and drips, and chattered at me, but I couldn't respond much.

I kept thinking—why *me*? I suppose everyone thinks this. But, hell, I never hurt anyone! I'd only slipped out for a few Leinenkugels and got nabbed by some maniac. The whole thing made me angry. If I could have talked I would have given all those doctors and nurses some lives of chill demigods like Caligula or Hitler or Dick Cheney—just to show them how being cold and alone really feels.

After a long time I was moved to a regular hospital room. Several times a day the nurses hauled me out of bed and made me walk up and down the hall while they held on to me. There really wasn't much to say, my jaw was sort of locked up, so I stayed quiet. I slept a lot and had strange dreams.

When this sort of thing is happening, it's just you and the darkness whispering mysteries back and forth. I recall one crazy dream: There was this big, abstract mural painting that was sliding over the ceiling and down the walls of my room—icebergs and frozen clouds oozing down sky blue walls. I watched for a long time and decided I would try and put myself *into* that painting. Maybe it would slide me all the way out of this hospital and I could get back to my lives.

I got out of bed and started feeling my way across the room toward the picture, canes in hand and dragging my rolling IV stand behind me, unplugging it from the wall as I moved. Out of my room I went and down the hall, following the painting as it slipped along the walls and ceiling. I was unable to understand why the nurses at the desk were so upset when they looked up and saw me. Suddenly they were grabbing at me and scolding, hustling me back to my bed.

"But those icebergs," I kept saying, "don't you see them? They're melting all over the place. There's going to be a flood. You better get some mops!"

"It's okay, Cyril," they said as they tucked me back in. "Don't get yourself worked up. You're going to be fine. Just don't be getting out of bed by yourself."

A lot of doctors came to look me over, sometimes whole parades, young and old folks in white jackets, asking me questions out of the dim light. It seems like I had survived some of the lowest body temperatures possible. Perhaps I'd set a new record.

I tried to point out the iceberg painting to them, but none of them could see it. They assured me that I was doing fine—amazingly well, they said, despite my itches and aches. In time I started to believe them. Then they asked me more questions. Instead of giving them answers, I tried to give them a few brief lives. These little biographies meant more than any facts I could give them, but they couldn't understand this—that my lives could be so meaningful. When I started one of my recitations, they would usually head for the door. I had a reputation: I was the man who apparently hadn't had much of a life, but represented everything with accounts of other people's lives.

How do you cure a guy of *this* strange affliction? Duct tape and aspirin, maybe a little Super Glue. Okay, I admit it, I am a strange case.

The sheriff and his deputy came to my bedside often and tried to ask me questions about Balaclava. Hell! I didn't know who that goddamned fur-face was, I told them—he was some monster who'd grabbed me! He'd driven off toward

Readstown after he'd stiffed the Mobil station and kidnapped me. Then he dumped me halfway in the snow, that's *all* I know, and it's enough!

Later the sheriff told me that Balaclava had forced another car off the road, causing it to spin out on the ice and crash into a tree. Two people had been badly hurt, but Balaclava kept going. He didn't care. He wounded a clerk in a robbery attempt near Knox, Illinois, so it seems like he really was headed toward Peoria. He doesn't care. Maybe his parents were alcoholics. God knows where he is now. Out there somewhere, a full-time pissed-off monster pointing that ultimate gat at people, threatening to pull the trigger and blast their faces off if they don't do as he tells them.

Some television people and big-time news reporters picked up on my story. When they found out what I had survived they started calling me on the phone at the hospital; one of the national networks sent a guy with a microphone and a whole camera crew to question me about my ordeal. I was the famous old guy who'd been dumped out of a truck by some hoodlum to die in a blizzard—then I almost made it all the way back home on my own. My story slipped onto the screens for a day among all the batterings, bombings, beheadings, and ballbustings. I was a sort of amusing relief from the slaughter, an old guy who had actually beaten death. How unusual and endearing.

A high-toned foundation in the East got wind of my tale and decided to give me its annual award for bravery. They called me on the telephone in my hospital room to grandly give me the news of their benevolence. Fifty thousand smackers, they said. Fifty thousand big ones just for stumbling around and almost getting frozen to death! Now *that's* bravery!

The dear, grand hearts even arranged to pay the taxes directly on their award to me, so that I cleared the whole $50,000. They invited me to rent formal clothes and attend their annual award banquet in New York at their expense. I would have been a hell of a curiosity—a bandaged twig in a tuxedo—but I couldn't make it. So they sent me their check anyway, express mail, fully insured, with a number on it. They arranged to have my picture taken holding it up in my bed. At the ceremony in New York, Mayor Bloomberg accepted the award in my name and said a few nice things about how some big stories could happen—even far out in the boonies, away from the *show*.

And that check—$50,000 it read! Fifty thousand clams—and it was the *real goods*. What does a poor, old, half-melted Klondike like me do with that kind of dough? I hadn't figured that out yet. But I didn't want to just stick it in some bank account. I wanted to take care of that dough myself, all those crinkly bills—I wanted to riffle them through my fingers—maybe once a month, and then hide them away again. Why should I give the wad to some bank bozo in a three-piece suit to punch in as numbers into his computer?

When the UPS guy brought the check to the hospital and asked me to sign and verify receipt, I recognized him from around town. This guy had never paid *any* attention to me before. One time I'd tried to tell him a life and he ignored me. But now you'd have thought I was the latest deluxe pizza. He even arranged to have his picture taken with me. When everybody was gone I just stuck the envelope in the drawer of my bed stand for a while and didn't talk to anybody about it—not even the Empress Theodora. More on this in a little while.

Later, when I got out of the hospital, I took the check to the little bank in Soldiers Grove and told them I wanted to cash it. Everybody stepped out of their glass cubicles to look at me like I was bananas. The bank director invited me to come into his office and had a quiet chat with me. He had all kinds of fancy ideas about how I could invest it or deposit it. But I insisted on the cash, and finally they agreed to do this for a small handling fee. It took them a few days to produce all that lettuce—500 one-hundred-dollar bills—that's how I wanted it; but eventually they came up with the whole load and I handed over the endorsed check.

I didn't know how to act as they counted out all that cash for me. When they had finished, I was numb. I asked, "Can you give me a paper bag?" They gave me a couple of big envelopes. My hands felt like they were burning when I took up all that moolah. I took the fat envelopes back to my room in the rest home and took a nap beside the cash; finally I stuffed it into two big old sweat socks, put them under my mattress and started trying to forget about them.

But that would be many weeks later. There was a pretty nurse who had the afternoon swing at the hospital. I've always been sort of flustered by women, but this one was so nice; just looking at her helped to warm me out of the perma-frost. I'd wake up from one of my naps and there she'd be, her beautiful face, as she gave me some kind of treatment, tapping my IV tubes with her fingernail, or giving me pills to take. I'd never learned how to flirt—but I thought maybe I could learn with her. It was best when she was taking my pulse and holding my wrist.

I always wanted to give her a life to think about. That's what I do best. I could think of a hundred beautiful women she resembled, but I had to get it just right. Finally I said to her, "I'm trying to figure out who you look like—maybe Dési-rée Clary, or Elinor Wylie. Is it Vera Hruba Ralston or Sigrid Hjertén?" I meant to flatter her, but she didn't know any of these names. She gave me her wonderful smile, though, and that was very nice.

Was I flirting okay? I wasn't sure, but I was trying hard to learn.

Another kind of young woman showed up by my bed one day with a clipboard; maybe she was twenty years old, but she acted like she was running the whole show. She looked kind of snippy like Bette Davis, but if I'd told her this she wouldn't have known who I was talking about. Anyway, she was too snooty to be given a life. I had no desire to flirt with this woman.

"Cyril," she said in her superior voice, "we don't seem to have any past records of you in the hospital. Have you been here before?"

Damn—I *hate* this new familiarity that young people have! No twenty-year-old snot has any business calling me by my first name! What kind of a world is this? Even though I might look like roadkill, I deserve *some* respect.

"My name is Mr. Solverson," I corrected her. "No, I have not been here before."

She blinked once when I corrected her, but went on. "We need some information, *Mr. Solverson.* Do you have insurance?"

"I'm a resident of the care home in Soldiers Grove. They have my insurance records."

"Do you have any information with you?"

I told her my billfold had been stolen by Balaclava.

"Your clothes are here in the locker. I'll make a list of your belongings and you can sign it. But do I have your permission to look in your wallet for your medical card, Mr. Solverson?"

"I told you, there's no wallet. It was taken by the man who abducted me."

"Do you remember your social security number?"

Now how the *hell* am I supposed to know my social security number while I'm lying on my frozen ass in a hospital bed, half out of my noggin?

"6086245731," I say off the top of what's left of my head. I think it's my phone number, but can't be sure; it is the only number I can remember for the moment—and it is good enough for this sniffy kid.

"Mr. Solverson, there are ten digits in that number. Social security has nine."

"How did *that* happen? There's mysteries *everywhere* around this place," I said in mock wonder.

"Maybe you'll remember later. Who is your next of kin?"

"I have none."

"Who is your nearest relative?"

"I have none."

"Can you give me the name of a close friend?"

"I have none."

"Surely there is some distant relative somewhere?"

I think hard, but I can think of no one. I decide to invent a relative so that this prissy missy will just go away.

Who would I like to be my distant relative? Lots of people. But today I think of . . . Thurman Tucker. He was a reserve outfielder for the Chicago White Sox and Cleveland Indians in the 1940s. He had a couple of pretty fair seasons for the Sox. He had a huge mouth like Joe E. Brown, and I saw a picture of him once in the *Sporting News* with half a dozen hardboiled eggs stuffed into his mouth. He wore steel-rimmed specs and I thought he looked like a pretty good guy. "Thurman Tucker," I said. I spelled it out for her.

"And what relationship is Thurman Tucker to you?"

"He is my cousin three times removed. He might even be deceased by now."

Pause. "Do you know his phone number?"

"011-43-6841."

"Cyril," she said. "That does not sound like a phone number. Is it your social security number?"

"You said you wanted nine numbers. My *name* is Mr. Solverson!"

"*Mr. Solverson*," the young woman's voice had gone very, very cold. A gap of about sixty years yawned and opened its abyss between us. "Where does Thurman Tucker live?"

"Did anyone ever tell you that you look like Eva Braun?" I asked her.

"Where does Thurman Tucker live, Cyril?"

"Do you want me to tell you about Eva Braun?"

"No, Mr. Solverson. Where does Mr. Tucker live?"

"France."

Pause. "There is no one in the United States who is close to you?"

"Balaclava."

"Who is that?"

"He's a gunman. He's the guy who almost aced me. Is that close enough?"

"Cyril!" she said wearily. "You need another nap, you're not being nice. I'll come back later," and she struts off, wriggling her officious butt.

Here I am laid out like frozen broccoli in a hospital, and she's bouncing around, trying to make me think of numbers I don't remember.

I suppose I should admit that young people generally piss me off these days. Maybe I should just say that I don't feel much connection. I can't recall much about being young—except that it wasn't pleasant. I remember hustling to avoid the loud brouhahas of my drunken parents, and trying to make myself invisible on school playgrounds that were more like prison yards. I remember being punched around in high school halls.

I did a lot of dreaming about other people's lives when I was young.

My memory has gone off the rails. I've been completely discombobulated by all that has happened to me—the abduction, the miracle of the policemen finding me in the snow, the saving of my life. All the drugs I take seem to shave off my ability to remember things.

I recall sneaking out of my room to go over to Burkhum's Tap and have a few beers. I remember talking to some people at the bar. Then I went out into the storm, ran into Balaclava and he pulled a gun on me that looked like a howitzer.

Then that bastard left me out in the blizzard. Maybe he was the one who shot off my toes before he sent me off in the snow. It's all became such a muddle—too much cold reality for me to deal with.

I was ill-tempered, just wanted all the probing, pricking, pilling, and questioning to stop. Suddenly, because of certain circumstances, some folks—after decades and years of not even knowing I existed—have decided that my life is now important enough for them to preserve.

There were chilblains on my hands and ear that were driving me nuts; they had to tie my hands back on the bedsides so I couldn't scratch or rub. The chilblains hurt like the very devil, but it was the ones that were on my feet that really set me off. I couldn't reach them, and they itched all the time so that I would start to howl. The nurses came in and scolded me, told me to stop making so much noise—I was disturbing other patients. I tried to get them to scratch my feet. I recited Job's life for them—all that stuff about sores and boils and suffering—but they didn't know who Job was.

I woke up one morning and Bonnie, the good nurse, was in my room holding my wrist, taking my pulse. Maria Montez? Gussie Moran? Alexandra Kollontai? I was still trying to think who she looked like so I could give her a life. I was running through some beautiful women in my mind. Then I got it for sure: "The Empress Theodora of Byzantium," I said out loud. "That's who you look like. Just like the mosaic of her on the wall of San Vitale at Ravenna."

"How's *that*?" Bonnie asked.

"She was the wife of Justinian, emperor of Byzantium, and then she got to be empress when he died. Pretty good for a gal whose old man was a circus bear keeper, who had to become an actress and occasionally take to working the streets just to make a few bucks. But one day Justinian saw her on the street and really got a load of how beautiful she was, and that was *it*. He couldn't think of anyone else. They had to rewrite the laws in Byzantium which stated that emperors could not marry actresses. Theodora was gorgeous but, much more than that, she was smarter than everyone else. Justinian used to take advice from her, and one time she convinced him to make a stand with his guards and save Byzantium from some bozos who were attacking the city. Everybody else had run away, but Justinian's guards were able to hold off the attackers. Theodora's advice had saved the most beautiful city in the world from being sacked. The Empress Theodora—that's who you look like, Bonnie. That's not too bad."

Bonnie listened to me carefully—not like some other people who get nervous or suspicious when I put a life on them—and she liked what she heard. I started calling her Theodora when she came into my room, and it always made her smile.

I told her lots of other lives and she always listened carefully as she checked my IV or took my temperature. Sometimes I'd be asleep when she came into my room to give me a treatment, and she would brush her fingertips on my cheek or the back of my hand. When I opened my eyes—there would be the sparkling face of Theodora. What a way to wake up! It was like a Sinatra song.

I started to act kind of strange. Lovesick is probably more accurate. A warmth in my cold body. A crush. By God, I had a senior crush! I didn't know what to do, but it was damned exciting, I was thinking fast, and I always think in lives.

Theodora especially liked to hear the lives of women, so one day I told her about Nila Mack: "She was born in a little town in Kansas around the turn of the twentieth century. She lost her parents early and got married to an actor when she was a very young woman. He taught her a lot about the stage. She went to New York with him and eventually got a job with the Columbia Broadcasting System. She impressed people and they decided they wanted to put her in charge of children's shows, and she became the first woman director at CBS. She put together a show using kid actors, called, *Let's Pretend*. She broadcast it on Saturday mornings; it became famous and ran for twenty years.

"When I was a kid I used to hide from my parents while they nursed their Saturday morning hangovers, and I'd listen to *Let's Pretend* on the white Philco in my room. Nila Mack had one story that she produced every year that became my favorite, about a big talking toad who loved a beautiful princess. That toad was so hideous the princess would run away whenever she saw him. But one day he managed to tell her that if she kissed him on the forehead something wonderful would happen. It took her awhile to work up to this—but one day the princess gave the toad a cautious kiss on his horny old forehead and he turned instantly into a handsome, rich prince who began praising her and proposing marriage."

I could tell that Theodora felt a little wary about what I was getting at with this story, so I held off for a couple of weeks. Then one Saturday morning, I said, "Theodora, it's time for *Let's Pretend*. All you have to do is give me a little smacker on my forehead, just to see what happens then."

She thought about this. Surely it was against the rules, and I'm not sure she really wanted to do it—but, God bless her, Bonnie bent her beautiful face down to mine and planted a light kiss on my forehead. I felt like I was being visited by the Holy Ghost.

"Well," she said, smiling down on me. "You're *still* Cyril."

"Look again," I said. "I'm happy and rich. I've got $50,000, and I've been kissed by the Empress Theodora of Byzantium! How many old guys can claim such stuff? I'm now a prince—but alas, too aged to propose marriage to you."

It almost broke my heart a few weeks later when Bonnie told me that she was moving to Milwaukee to go to graduate school.

But all of this was good preparation for my meeting Louise. But I'll tell more about this later.

When they finally let me out of that hospital, I'm still wearing bandages, and my skin looks like rancid cheese. I have to use two canes because of the toes I'd lost, and I can only hear out of my left ear. I'd always had a touch of arthritis, but now it came on like the Inquisition.

My hands look like two wild turkey heads; I sometimes have to use elastic bands around my knuckles and fingers—and I'm cold all the time, sometimes wear an old overcoat even when it's warm outside. When I lurch around in the care home I must look like a flag pole about to collapse. But by God, I'm still moving—can still stick one foot in front of the other with the help of my crutches—and I've been kissed by the Empress Theodora. How many old guys can claim such a thing?

On occasions now when everything is hurting all over my body, I'm not sure—if I'd had a choice—that I would have allowed those docs to save my ass. But those guys don't give you any choice about that if they see any light in your eyes. It's their work. Somewhere inside me there seems to be a little furnace that those medical people were able to locate and stoke up again to wake me out of that cold void.

My skin was gray all over until they got the fluids moving and then I began to get a little color. I had some clots in blood vessels that they busted up with medicine. A few of the trickier ones they got with some kind of rays from a machine. They had to get my hands and feet and ear and cheeks and chin and nose going again—all those things that got frozen. They were tinkering around with my heartbeat, too. All this kept me in bed for a long time. Sometimes it was touch and go, but I was hanging on to everything I could. I didn't want to end up like Johnny Eck, the old carnie freak show guy with half a body. I need more than that.

It was a long haul, and I lost some parts along the way: One ear, four toes, and the little and ring fingers on my left hand. Somehow I managed to hang on to my pecker. They wanted to do something about my frozen nose, too—but I said no, no, no—just work with what you've got. Can you imagine an old guy in my shape, being that vain? But it wasn't vanity—I just wanted to hang on to my faithful proboscis that had breathed so many breaths for me over the years. So they did their best to just keep it going. Now it looks like a wad of chopped sirloin stuck on my mug—but it still works.

I'm not sure how the residents in the senior care home feel about my returning—the old fool who was always babbling about other people's lives. Most of them couldn't hear what I was saying anyway. I thought I detected some heavy sighing when they rolled my wheelchair into the entry hall.

Now at the care home, there are times when it seems like I can feel that $50,000 still smoldering under me as I take a nap. Once in a while I take the bills out and riffle the stacks like decks of cards. But mostly, I don't think about that money anymore. And those big-time media folks—they never checked in with me again. They are swarming over other stories.

As for Balaclava, I don't know what happened to him. But I don't think they've tracked him down yet. He's out there somewhere with his pipe gun and slit of a mouth. He doesn't care about anything. I wonder how many guys there are in the world like Balaclava? It makes my gonads turn cold if I think about it.

Balaclava

Balaclava is driving hard with the winds of the snow-storm as he motors east on US Route 14 toward Madison, watching the myriad flakes twirl down toward his face in the headlights, and clump together on the windshield until wiper blades sweep them aside. The drive is becoming even more dangerous and he has to be certain he doesn't drive off into pallid oblivion. Too many numbing hours in the cold white. He's got to find coffee soon and something to eat.

The blizzard is massive; according to the truck radio it stretches across the whole upper Midwest from Minnesota, Wisconsin, Iowa, Illinois, past Indiana into Ohio. It jolts his truck with terrific, head-on gusts, and his arms are numb from wrestling the wheel. Balaclava knows his way through hard weather, but he also knows his limitations. Something stupid is going to happen if he doesn't soon stop pushing himself.

No cars or pickups are on the road now, only a few big rigs occasionally whoosh past him, locked in a differential gear, going the other way, west. If one of those guys falls asleep and starts drifting out of the night over into his lane he'll end up tomato paste.

This stupid pickup that he'd cross-wired in Winona has only front-wheel drive. Hopefully he will be able to dump it for something better at his next stop—a truck that can really pull in this weather. What kind of an idiot was he becoming? He should have paid more attention to what he was stealing in Minnesota. Front-wheel drive! The heater doesn't work well either, and a pickup without a load in its bed in this hard weather is so light it's like a butterfly on ice.

But the blizzard is great cover—and Balaclava is very good at disappearing in hard weather, pulling the storm over his head like a blanket. Once he gets himself rolling he can become very hard to find. But sometimes when he makes mistakes or pushes himself too hard he digs his hole deeper.

He doesn't want to end up stranded tonight like that jabbering geezer back there in Wisconsin who he pushed out into the storm, peeing his pants and trying to trudge through the drifts. Jesus, what an old cuckoo the guy was—and what a way to go! Balaclava snorts out a chuckle when he thinks about that old fart stumbling through the storm, probably babbling some lives to God, trying to give the Big Man some lessons on how to spare his miserable carcass from this whiteout. The world is full of old gizzards dealing out twaddle, but this one was seriously nuts.

The snow in his lane is only about three or four inches deep now, so Balaclava knows a snowplow has been through not too far ahead, but he's got to stop soon. Now he is the one who has to take a very serious piss—and he is hungrier than a bitch owl in heat. Eventually he sees some lights coming up on the right side of the road through the driving snow. Whatever that goddamned place is, it will have to be the one. If it's a motel or convenience store, he'll break in and take whatever he needs. And he's got to change vehicles soon.

He starts pumping his brakes and eases the truck onto an entry road, turning his lights out as he slows down, so as not to announce his arrival. But no one has plowed this small strip of road surface—the snow is deep, and the incline steeper and longer than he thought. There must be ice under the snow because the truck starts going sideways and he can't stop it from slipping all the way around, still sliding, sideways again, raising his short hairs as he still spins, whirling all the way around again, two figure-eights, before it stalls in the drifts, the rear end slipping down into a ditch. The motor is ticking and there is nothing but headlong snow outside his windshield. *Son of a bitch!*

Breathing hard, he gathers his wits and tries the ignition again. The motor kicks back on, and for the first time he's glad he has front-wheel drive because, by rocking the vehicle, he is able to inch the truck's rear end up out of the ditch through the drifts, and ease it very slowly the rest of the way down the slope into the parking lot.

He's shaky. He could have been chopped liver back there stuck in those drifts. He's got to be more careful. Just the slightest mistake and he'd be out walking in the drifts like that old geezer. But he's in luck again, he sees that the lights come from a little restaurant bar with a small attached motel. There's a heavy Dodge pickup parked outside with a snowy load of firewood in its bed and a blade attached on the front.

He pulls into the back of the parking area, steps out urgently without slamming his door, immediately unzips his fly, takes out his cock and pisses a tremendous stream downwind. He studies the windows of the café as his bladder empties. Only one man seems to be in the place, probably the cook and owner, sitting at the counter, reading a newspaper. The guy hasn't heard the truck come in above the noise of the storm.

Balaclava sizes him up. That is the stupid son of a bitch who did not plow out his entry road and almost hung me up for good. He glares across the lot through the window. That is a dipshit who deserves to bite it.

It all looks like easy pickings. This goddamned, fucking cook seems to be alone. Balaclava stands at a distance and studies the place some more before he unhooks his big fur hat at the chin and pushes the flaps up off his cheeks. He is still simmering about almost hanging himself up on the entry road. Everything is a hard chance for him these days, but pulling into a road-stop entryway should not be such a challenge.

He strides heavily through the snow to the restaurant and shoves the door open with a crash. Huge in his ugliness, startling and fierce in his snow-covered coat and strange furry hat, Balaclava rolls into the room like a jagged iceberg.

The cook jumps up, his newspaper flops to the floor and he backs up six feet from the counter. "Hey, wow, you almost knocked me out of my tree!" he blurts uneasily, backing up still another six feet. "I wasn't expecting no one out in this howler."

He gives Balaclava a wary quick study up and down. "Let me pour you some coffee, stranger," he says. Nice and easy, he says this. He goes for the pot on his machine. While he is doing this, Balaclava sits down on a metal stool, leans forward onto the counter, slides his pant leg up over his boot top with his hand, and reaches into the long pouch along his ankle to bring out his considerable gun and place it on the counter in front of him.

When the guy comes back with a cup and the coffee pot, he is asking, "Cream and sugar?" But then he sees the weapon on the counter and stops. "My God! What is that? A bazooka?"

Balaklava responds slowly, "This is something that would blow out all your teeth and ram them back like bullets through your brain, my friend. It would also take out the lower part of your nose, both your cheeks, and your Adam's apple. Your head might hang by a shred, but your own mother wouldn't even recognize you. It's loaded.

Best do what I say, pal. I am really pissed! I almost killed myself sliding down your fucking entry road. Why didn't you plow it out?"

"Jesus, I'm sorry, sorry. It's such a hell of a night out there. I did clear it earlier, but I never expected anyone to be coming in here in this storm. It was lazy of me. I'm sorry!" He looks at the blunderbuss on his counter again. "Please take it easy." He sets the empty cup in front of the weapon. His hand is shaking and he slops a bit of coffee onto the counter.

Balaclava heaves himself off the stool and snatches his gun away from the hot puddle. "Goddamn it! Watch it, you idiot!" He aims the weapon at the cook's head. "Is there anybody else around this place? Are there guests in the motel?"

"No, sir, nobody else is here." The cook is close to fainting, expecting death at any moment, clutching his arms around himself, backing off again, almost falling down backward.

Balaclava is disgusted. "Look, asshole. I need food. I need it right now. I don't need you shitting your pants or spilling coffee all over the place."

"I hear you talkin'!" the cook says, stepping backward some more.

"You got any weapons around here? Don't fuckin' lie to me! I know you do."

"I got a little pistol under the tray in the cash drawer. That's all I got, and I'm not going anywhere near it. You got the big gun, brother. You win. Whatever you want. I got three kids and my wife's pregnant. I don't have much money in the register, but you can have it all. If you want food, it's on the house."

"You better believe it is. I want a half dozen fried eggs, a triple order of hash-browns, ten strips of bacon, five slices of white toast, and you can bring the coffee pot over here and leave it while you're cooking. Don't press any buttons or go into your pocket for your cell phone. Don't go into the back room. I'll blow your fuckin' head off, junior! Got that? Just cook on the grill. I'll be watching."

"I ain't going to do nothing but what you say," the cook says. "Comin' right up just the way you like them. Best eggs and bacon you ever had. I'm just going to reach to this shelf up here and get my big skillet down. Okay? Then I'm going to get the eggs and bacon out of the fridge. You can watch me all the way. Just take it easy."

After eating, Balaclava feels better. He hadn't realized how hungry he was. The food was good and it seemed to soothe him. He decided not to blow the cook's head off.

As he scarfs down the last of the eggs and potatoes, Balaclava thinks about taking a few winks in one of the beds in the motel. Maybe the storm would ease off a bit if he slept a few hours. But what the hell would he do with this simple-minded shit while he slept? Chain him to another bed? Somebody else might come in from the highway into the restaurant—if they could make it down the idiot's driveway.

He could blow the cook away and then take a room, but somebody else might come in. The guy was cooperating, cooked decent eggs. In the end Balaclava just rips the phone out, cuts the long chord off, and makes the guy give over his cell phone.

"Now, your truck keys."

"They're in my coat pocket over there on the hook," the cook points.

Balaclava levels his gun on the cook again. "You get 'em, friend. Don't do anything funny when you reach in your pocket or they'll be scraping your brains off the menu board."

The man jingles his keys out of the coat pocket and puts them into Balaclava's extended hand.

"Now, pal, you and me are going outside." Balaclava buttons his heavy coat again and motions with his pistol for the cook to go out the door. At the curb there is a "Senior Citizens" parking sign on a metal post. He pushes the man down against it and cinches his legs and hands tight to the base of the post with the long phone cord. He considers gagging him, but figures he'll just let the guy do his singing to the storm. It must be about zero degrees and the wind is up.

Balaclava goes back into the café. There is a big display box of beef jerky packages on the register counter and he stuffs two huge handfuls into his coat pockets, takes the money and small revolver from under the cash drawer. He finds a container of cleanser spray and covers everything he's touched while he's been in the restaurant and mops a bit with a bar towel. He locates a toolbox under the counter and takes a hammer. He finds the main switchboard just inside a closet door and throws off all the lights indoors and out. No one will even know this place is here in the dark for a few days until the storm moves out. He takes the big flashlight from under the counter.

As a last thought he removes the cook's coat from the hook behind the counter and, on his way out, drops it over the guy's shoulders. "That's for the eggs and bacon," he says. Already the cook, shivering in his sweater, is barely able to lift his head, but his eyes are wide and beseeching and his pupils focus on Balaclava. He tries to say something, but it doesn't come out right. Children, wife—something.

Hell with him. He should have plowed his fucking entry road.

Balaclava tells him, "Maybe somebody else will come sliding down your road, shithead. At least I'm giving you that chance."

There is half a tank of gas in the Dodge and it starts right up with the key. While the truck is warming he slips out of the cab again, goes to the rear and bangs on the license plate with the hammer until it crumples and folds up under the chrome bumper like someone had accidentally bumped it hard backing up against something. Then he gives it a few more licks to obscure the number a bit more.

Balaclava climbs back in, turns the truck around toward the exit, revs it a bit, pops the clutch and takes a hard run up the ramp. The truck has good muscle. The out ramp isn't as steep as the entrance and the snow not quite so deep. In a moment he has plugged out onto the road and settled into the plowed highway lane as he heads east again with the driving storm.

Chapter 4

Louise

I have requested no roommate and pay extra for this privacy. I had the mover/helpers bring a few boxes of my carefully selected books from the farm, my tape player, a large plastic container of music cassettes, and my teapot.

My room is like an overgrown child's room; it smells of long inhabitance, of diapers and age-old sweat. There is a small desk—maybe suitable for doing high school homework—a hard wooden chair, an alcove with a toaster, electric water heater, microwave oven, and some odd pieces of crockery on a shelf. Thank heaven there is a small section of bookshelves built into a wall, and in the divider between the kitchen and living area. The shelves are shallow, intended for knickknacks, but I lay my books in sideways and jam most of them in. The rest I line up between bookends on the dresser and a small table.

When they checked me into my room, a small television was already tuned to *General Hospital* for me. I switched it off. The little bathroom seems clean and there are many handles and grab bars around the shower and tub to hold onto. There is the bed, a long couch, a severe looking easy chair, and a rack by the door where I can keep my cane, umbrella, and walker, and hang my few hats.

My window looks out on a large parking lot, with a few small patches of trees clustered here and there on islands in the asphalt. I was introduced to some of my fellow residents as I was wheeled in. They seemed dear people in various stages of separation. The lobby and sitting room are already decorated for Christmas with a brightly bedecked tree, an illuminated Santa Claus who winks and blinks a red nose, a crèche with kneeling idolaters and a bouncing baby Jesus.

Left alone in my room at last, after signing more papers and receiving more instructions, I sit down in the plain chair and consider suicide, which is what I imagine most people do at this point of their arrival. But like most people, I haven't the courage or the means to do the deed properly. I have only this sinking feeling.

I am quiet for a long, long time in the chair, my eyes open but seeing nothing—then finally I stir to regard the bed. I am drifting dismally. It is time for a nap, the staple of my life, and so I make my way over and lie down on the tufted spread, pulling up a light blanket, allowing unconsciousness to sustain me for a while.

But when I awaken after harsh dreams I am disoriented and irritable. What have I done to myself? The red light dot of the fire alarm blinks occasionally high over the entry door. I try to time its signal, but soon lose interest. The electric heater turns on low and clicks as evening light fades from the window.

I rise and shuffle to the chair again and put on a tape of a Vivaldi concerto, but it does not occupy me at this time. I go to the desk, take some of the care home stationery and begin a letter to my cousin in France. What can I say to him? *Dear André, I have institutionalized myself—please come and save me?* Then I remember that André died two years ago. I had been devastated because I was unable to travel to his funeral in France. He was the last of my relatives. I weep quietly as I remember this.

Someone is calling out feebly in the hallway—someone fallen—and I hear hurried steps and professionally comforting voices. The sound of some visitor's motorcycle roaring into the parking lot is like the charge of some great animal.

There is a knock on the door. "Louise," a voice calls, and the knob shakes—but I have turned the key in the lock. "It's time to come for dinner, Louise. Do you need help?"

"No, I'm fine. I'll be along," I say.

I rise and go to the bathroom, splash water on my face, run a comb through my gray hair.

I will not weep beyond this room. My tears are mine, not to be shown to others.

The dining room is large, and there is only hushed conversation, except for one woman standing, leaning on her hands spread before her on her table. Apparently she believes it is her job to sing and entertain the others during meals. Or at least this is what *she* believes—I'm not sure if she has officially been assigned this duty, but she sings, slightly off key and full-throated, an old song I remember hearing on the radio in the late forties and early fifties, quite popular then when Heath and I first came to live on our farm in Wisconsin. "Together," it is called:

> *We strolled the lane together*
> *Laughed at the rain together . . .*

No one pays any attention to the woman, but I realize that this is her *work* and she is going to help us all with her song, providing us with dinner music.

I sit down at an empty table with my eyes lowered, but am soon joined by several others as the food carts are rolled between the tables, and trays distributed. I nod a greeting to my tablemates, but they do not notice. One woman, even older than I, hugs a Raggedy Ann doll, and places it beside her on the chair as she eats, occasionally offering the doll a morsel. "She just doesn't get enough to eat!" she declares with some concern to others at the table.

Chicken breasts, peas, french fries, a flaccid salad. An ancient man at our table, his head bent inches over his plate, eats the peas with his fingers one at a time. "You're new," the woman next to me says. "The chicken's always just half done," she warns me. "Salmonella," she whispers conspiratorially. The singer has her head raised:

> You're gone from me
> But in my memory,
> We always will be together.

She concludes her song. It is such a silly, sentimental old song, sung so shakily, but I applaud her. The others around the room look at me as if I am insane. The singer is surprised, but smiles graciously in my direction, as an old entertainer might do. I go to my ill-cooked chicken, and she begins another song. There is some talk at our table, but it is lightly passed—weather, the Green Bay Packers, the ghastly food, a recent death amongst the residents. As a newcomer I am not expected to participate. I eat a few spoonfuls of the tapioca dessert, and return to my room.

I miss Heath, I miss our trees, I miss the birds and fields, the comfort of my long shelves of books, the sun and rain through changing seasons; I miss France all those years ago—when peace had come and freedom, the release from threat, the future extending with a fresh glow into my youth.

There is a knock at my door. I rise to turn the key. My medications have arrived from the pharmacy. Would I need assistance in arranging my pillbox?

Not today, thank you. No.

Do I have enough blankets?

Yes, it would seem so.

The door closes. The red dot of the fire alarm blinks exactly every two minutes over the door. I have been able to figure this out. Thirty of these blinks and an hour has passed.

I begin a rereading of *Eugénie Grandet*, until I feel too sleepy to read and lie down fully clothed, pulling a blanket up over me from the foot of the bed. Perhaps I will change to my pajamas later.

CHAPTER 5

Cyril

I am a different person in my room now that I've come back from the hospital. I stumble and thump things; it is an adventure to get up, sit down, go to the can, lie down, sit in a chair, or even scratch what's left of my nose. That son of a bitch, Balaclava, really set me back. So I try to stay still, hoping that my faithful body cells are laboring in there to pull things back together for me; but I find it difficult to even wrap my mind lightly around a life or two. Things have gotten a little mixed up—and this makes me nervous.

Sitting up makes my back hurt. Mostly I stay in bed—like Proust, Oblomov, Don Juan, and Casanova, I spend a lot of time in the sack. But what bothers me most is that my mind seems buggered, too, so I fight hard to keep things straight. I can't let things start to slip. I figure if I lose control of the lives, they might start running together, sliding over into each other, and I'll be deep in the wallow.

What will happen to me then? I'll become a black hole. I try to think good thoughts. Maybe if all the lives come washing and mixing together they'll become one perfect life—or maybe even one very bad life? How would things stack up? This is too serious for me to think about in my weakened state.

Cyril, get your ass in gear! Shake it out! Hang on to what you've got.

Three times a week they haul me off with a bunch of lurching elder residents to a physical therapy class in the medical center. Each of us is given a special exercise assignment. It's all figured out by computers as near as I can tell. Many of the other patients have wracked up their backs or legs in farm accidents. Others are cursed with arthritis or gout. Everyone does a separate task. I'm the only iceman in the class.

The exercise attendants are all staring into computers behind the counter when our group arrives. There are a half dozen of them. The screens somehow tell these folks what exercise programs to assign to each of us. The attendants rarely look up, and the lights from their computer screens give their faces a sinister glow. "Cyril," one of them says without looking up. "You start with five minutes on limbering machine number two, then move to rolling track number five and do ten minutes at .05 speed."

"Point zero five!" I say to him, acting like I'm in shock, trying to liven this joint up a bit. "Who do you think I am—Paavo Nurmi?"

"Who's Paavo Nurmi?" one of them asks. Oh-oh—I can see it on all their faces—their sudden realization that they've accidentally tripped my mechanism again.

I lean forward on the administration desk. They lower their heads and descend more deeply into their computer screens. "Paavo Nurmi. It's amazing how a guy that great can be forgotten. In 1924 he won five gold medals in the Paris Olympics. Five! The Flying Finn, they called him. The French went nuts over him. Everybody did. He'd run with a stopwatch in his hand to pace himself. Once on the same day he won the 1,500- and 5,000-meter races. Same day! That was in the time before antiaging foods and drinks and performance enhancement drugs. In those days you had to pull a race on just your own breakfast eggs.

"Nobody'd ever seen anyone like Paavo Nurmi. He had wheels! In 1928 when he was thirty-one he came back to the Olympics in Amsterdam and won the 10,000-meter race and pulled second in the 5,000 and the 3,000-meter steeplechase.

"At one point he held the world records for 1,500, 5,000, and 10,000 meters and one, three, six, and ten miles—*all* at one time. That is chugging, brother! That's like Sugar Ray Robinson winning the middleweight title five times after he'd held the welterweight title for years. Do you know who Sugar Ray Robinson was?" I figure all these physical therapists might know some lives of athletes.

But, "Naw, Cyril," one of them says abruptly without looking up from his screen. "*You*'ve got to get chugging though. Get yourself up on that machine." All of them are totally unimpressed that I am able to hold this stuff in my mind. They just want me to do painful exercises.

I heard one of them mutter an aside to another when I was in the gym last time. "Watch out, here comes the Google Man."

Google Man! It's true, they really don't need to have me blathering at them. Anything I hold in my head could be brought up by a couple of clicks on their keyboards. Their faces are lined up and staring at the screens like a crate of blighted lemons in their mysterious light.

So I go off to ease my suffering butt onto the seat of the limbering machine, which is like an upside-down spider. You pull on its legs with your hands and push down on its palps with your feet, and it runs poison up your ass as you pump. A man can't think straight when he's using all his energy like this.

All you can do is gaze up at the soaps on the TV screens, and hope for the best. There's no sound coming from the TV, but there is always some very tense situation going on with those young actors in the dramas. They all look like they need a laxative.

By the time I've shagged my ass at .05 for ten minutes on number five machine, it's time for all of us to crawl back to the minibus and be driven back to the home for lunch. I can't talk because my tongue's hanging out, and the rest of my fellow exercisers don't look to be in much better shape. But we have done our duties.

For lunch it is mac and cheese, green beans and a salad. There's a new tenant sitting in the chair next to me. She looks mighty woeful and she doesn't speak to anyone as she eats.

This care home is not exactly *Romper Room*—everyone is generally in a sky blue funk when they're first rolled in here. As I shovel in my mac and cheese I'm trying to think of something nice to say to my neighbor that might give her some cheer. She's a real pretty woman with her short white hair and slender hands.

I've never known how to talk much to women, but this is one I'd really like to talk to. *Cyril, I say to myself, you dope, don't get nervous and start blathering—just say something cool to her! Look at her—she's elegant. Don't just spout some empty-headed crap. Maybe you could give her an interesting life to think about.*

I'm not good at this sort of thing, never learned how to be smooth, but I try to display a little class when I speak to her. "My name is Cyril," I say. "Are you familiar with Christine de Pisan? You remind me of her."

She blinks only once. I can see she's surprised by my question—but she is thinking. I'm not used to people mulling over what I say to them! Then she starts talking: "Christine de Pisan was a medieval woman, the daughter of a Bolognese astrologer, very beautiful and witty, wrote poems and even a chronicle of Charles V.

"I was born in France, and where I'm from it is part of our history that Christine came to visit her daughter in the priory at Poissy near where my family home was. She wrote poems about her visit and left important details of how young, cloistered women lived."

I almost fall out of my chair. My mouth is open, my sore eyes are wide. I am numbed, unable to respond. No one has *ever* answered one of my questions and given a life back to me.

I struggle for breath, so surprised that I am speechless. A moment of moments. If I could get down on my dubious knees I would kneel before her.

Finally . . . finally I manage to utter, "Will you marry me?"

CHAPTER 6

Louise

I read as much as my challenged eyes will permit, I spend many hours listening to music, but I want to do this selectively, not merely perform these things as rote activities. I want to really listen, so I parcel out my limited energy. At times I sit in my stern chair and look at my framed reproduction of "Mme Manet on a Blue Couch" which I had hung on the wall. I cherish the cobalt color of her settee, and the way Mme looks so knowingly, almost impatiently, at the painter. *Hurry up!* she seems to say.

Sometimes I lie on the bed and dredge through remembered pieces of my life hour after hour. There's no order to my rambling—a memory of a small event comes into my mind for no particular reason, or something reminds me of something else. My eyes might be open, but I am taking a nap, a sort of open-eyed coma, and my dreams wash together with bits of reality; my unconsciousness is always odd and unrelated until it startles me back into cognizance. There is the good—and the bad—the frightening connections and the warm fancies.

I don't have to plan things anymore—or concern myself with what needs to be *done*. *Nothing* needs to be done—except that I must be cautious so as not to fall down, take my medicine on time, go to the bathroom regularly, and appear in the dining hall at meal times.

I don't wish to descend permanently into the television screen all my waking hours as so many of my coresidents do. So far I have been able to resist this.

I *know* what lies ahead—an event not to be overly pondered. So I strike sparks off my past, wondering why I did this thing or that thing. I think of a particular event and wonder what it *really* meant when it happened. Now that I have time to think about them, I recall places in my life where I turned a corner when I did not even realize I had done so, or how I could have saved myself great trouble if only I had only done a certain thing. There are the lovely memories, too, of young infatuation, a good bottle of wine, many moments and realizations in art, an éclat amongst the trees in our woods, a fine book, a walk with Heath, a moment of lovemaking, a vegetable triumph in the garden, a picture, a poem, a dance, some music that illuminated and sustained my life.

At last I have lived enough of my life so that I have some *wisdom* to rely on, knowledge I have accumulated to influence my decisions, some things that could possibly be useful to others, too. But no one really cares or consults with me about anything, and I am given no real decisions to make. It seems that things have already been decided *for* me. No wisdom is required in the face of this reality—nor, it seems to me, is wisdom much valued.

No one comes to see me in the home. Heath and I had been a hermitic twosome over our decades together, had only a few friends, and mostly these are all dead or doomed now. We had a few good neighbors who occasionally looked in on us, but basically we were by ourselves. I have no relatives with whom I am in touch; they all eventually disappeared into my vaporous memories of France across the sea when I was a girl. Heath's parents had both died suddenly when he was twelve and his only brother passed away a decade ago.

Heath and I had our fields, our woods, our work, our house, and each other.

We belonged to no groups or clubs, went to no meetings, rarely dined in the local bars and grills. We did not hunt our land, nor did we permit others to hunt it—and this, too, set us apart from our neighbors.

In late autumn the guns come out in the driftless hills, and the war with animals commences in full. I would begin to hear gunfire and it always conjured up terrifying memories of the war combat in France when I was a child. Heath would be off doing his chores, and I would be frightened that some stray shot might take him down. I was unable to walk in our woods when this bellicose activity was commencing. When we went to town for our groceries there were deer strung up like lynch victims from trees around the houses, and pickups with bloodied animals' corpses slung onto their beds as if they were firewood. This, too, stirred terrible memories for me and had its deep effect on me particularly, reinforcing our solitude.

Dearest Heath, this was his childhood home and these things had been part of his growing up, but he changed his customs for me as an act of love, knowing that hunting bewildered and appalled me. If he saw hunters straying onto our land he would emphatically order them to leave.

The caregivers in this home are professional and dedicated, but they are challenged and sometimes annoyed with their work. Like most people who labor in institutions that serve particular types of human beings—teachers, prison guards, ward nurses, military officers—they sometimes become impatient, especially when residents become querulous. Elders might be quiet people, but we are diverse; our one common denominator is that we are all moving now with varying speeds toward an inevitable conclusion, and our attitudes about this vary as we wobble toward our respective ends. At times we become overdemanding of our caregivers and impatient with each other, creating situations that are not productive.

Even though I dislike being here in this crowded, odiferous place, I have taken a personal vow: I swear I will be cooperative and patient with fellow residents and show gratitude to my caregivers. Otherwise I will become a living misery.

◦◦◦

I HAVE met a new resident—or I guess I should say an old resident—who apparently has returned to the home after what must have been a very serious episode in the hospital. He had been injured in some terrible way, perhaps not by fire—but by ice; an odd man who looks like a partially unwrapped mummy with his bandages. I feel concern for him, and he interests me because his mind is active. He asked me a strange, obscure question when he sat beside me at lunch, to which—by some wild chance—I was able to give him a full response. He was so astounded and apparently delighted by my answer to his question that he suddenly proposed marriage.

Of course, I ignored his proposal, but I must, however, advise him later to be more careful about such frivolities. Old women can be very dangerous—in ways different than younger ones.

CHAPTER 7

Cyril

Here I am—a seventy-nine-year-old mossback who's never had a date.

There she is—a woman like no other I've ever seen. And she actually pays attention to me. Is she just being kind to me? Her name is Louise. I want to know her better. I am attracted to her. How the hell do I do this?

Is this the beginning of love? Is that what this feeling I am feeling is? How would I know? What do I do now? Maybe I could invite her to sneak out for a beer with me. I've got to do this right. If she turns me down now I may never come out of my room again.

It's time for lunch in the dining room. I oil my boots, slather on Lilac Vegetal after cutting myself while shaving. I've got to remember to pull the bloody patch of toilet paper off my chin before I leave the room. I keep slicking down my few gray hairs and looking in the mirror.

What I see is not good. No, not good at all. I look like a lump of suet with Band-Aids on it. Why did I wait this long in my life to try and make a date with a woman?

I get out my best shirt, a blue and red plaid flannel that might catch her eye. If I had a car I'd invite her out to the Readstown Inn for brats and fried cheese curds. Maybe she would like that. I wonder if she likes beer? I've got to be careful with this kind of thing. I don't want to put her off, or make her think I am some kind of country goof.

She said she had been born in France and her name is Louise. That's pretty swishy, it seems to me. *Don't screw it up, Cyril!* Go slow. Think what Adolphe Menjou would do. Maybe I should grow a moustache so I could twirl it. Adolphe always moved slowly and was very elegant. I remember him in *The Sheik*, and he was in *One Hundred Men and a Girl* when he played Deanna Durbin's old man. He was cool and courtly, never pushed it.

Cyril, you don't want to make any fast moves! Nice and easy for old folks. Don't be talking with your mouth full—and make sure your fly is zipped. *Cultivated.* That's the word. Cover your mouth when you sneeze, and don't say "ain't."

She must have lived in the driftless hills to be staying in this care home, but I've never seen her around town. I would have noticed her. I'll get to the dining hall early and watch to see where she sits, then slip in at her table. How should I start talking to her again? I've never done this before.

I've listened to many lines over the years in Burkhum's Tap: "Weren't you in my high school class?" or "Haven't I seen you around Walmart's?" or "Hello, sugar, would you please pass the popcorn?" I don't think any of these would work with Louise. Adolphe Menjou would take her hand, kiss it, and say, "*Madame, enchanté.*" I don't think I could pull off that sort of thing either.

I watch her come into the dining room and she picks a table where no one is sitting. I'm a little shaky, but I suck it up, go over and sit down next to her. I'm nervous as hell, start playing with the silverware, and gaze off across the room as if I'm thinking about something important.

They're serving wieners and beans and slaw in the dining room. She nibbles at her slaw. I am trying to look cool as I cut a hotdog with my table knife, rather than use my fork. But I haven't a clue what to say to her.

The singing woman who entertains is offering "A Tree In the Meadow" today for our lunchtime pleasure. She's still way off-key, but I pretend to listen. Kate Smith used to sing that song. She was a big gal, from Duluth I think, and her manager was Ted something, and sometimes she would sing the national anthem before World Series games, but I'm so nervous I can't get anything straight right now. I go on poking at my beans in silence.

Louise takes the heat off me: "They should serve wine with these meals," she says with a chuckle. "It might make them more edible."

I know she's kidding, but I don't know how to respond to this and my mouth is full of hotdog. She's so trim and beautiful, she has that little French accent, and now she wants wine with her food. This mention of alcohol gives me, I think, a possible lead-in. My voice goes up three decibels as I ask her, "Do you like Leinenkugel?"

Damn it! Cyril, you stupid fossil, what a dumb thing to ask her! I wish I could swallow the whole sentence back like a cartoon character might swallow his balloon back. I can't believe I said it! I'm so ashamed my whole body starts itching,

But the lady is kind; she takes it up immediately without blinking an eye. "Well, my husband used to drink a bottle of Leinenkugel when he came in from the fields. I sometimes tasted his. It's not bad, as these things go, but I have to admit I haven't yet learned to favor beer very much." She even gives me a little smile. "But I could try."

I am a gone coon. I'm gulping. I am *sailing!*

Finally I manage to calm myself a bit. We sit and chat, the two of us, until the servers start clearing things away. I consider giving her a few lives, but have the good sense to keep off that. I don't want to scare her, so we talk about the home, the weather, the food and other stuff. Finally they are wiping off the table in front of us, so we have to leave. I say, "Can I walk you back to your room?"

"That would be nice," she says. Both of us use our canes as we trundle through the halls. When we reach her door I don't pull a Menjou *enchanté* act—but I at least have the presence to say, "I sure enjoyed talking to you."

"And I, too," she says, and smiles so sweetly again I almost fall down on the hall carpet. She goes into her room, and shuts the door. I'm ready to dance a jig on my frostbitten legs. I'm glittering—old busted, bandaged Cyril—all the way back to my room.

Was that a date? I did it okay. Cyril, you *really* did it. Casanova, Warren Beatty, Rudolph Valentino, Lord Byron, move over! Cyril is moving onto the scene.

When I get back in my room I step into the john to take a pee and see in the mirror that the blood-spotted patch of toilet paper is still stuck to my chin. I am going to have to work very hard to improve myself.

CHAPTER 8

Louise

The man with the bandages is recovering from nearly freezing to death—I found this out from some of the residents. Apparently he was abducted by some rogue and left for dead on a roadside in a driving blizzard. He must be very willful and strong to have endured such a crisis. He seems to enjoy talking to me. He is an odd combination of countryman and scholar, a serious collector of obscure facts about the lives of people.

I have taken several after-dinner strolls with him now and, though he is very shy, I find him to be more intriguing than other people I've met in the home, who seem overwhelmed by age and physical problems. But Cyril—that is his name, he told me—despite his grievous injuries, is still outgoing and ongoing, and determined to recover. He is still interested in things. I like his innocence and sanguinity. It is a rarity in this atmosphere.

And he says such odd things. The other day he told me that I looked like Thomas Hardy's second wife, Florence. Now *where* in heaven's name do you suppose he conjured that one? He says I have a round face like hers and remain essentially unsmiling, but that I seem to be a devoted person, as Florence Hardy was—and that I have visions.

My face is not round. I might be a sleepy-looking old woman, but I have no visions. Besides, Florence Hardy was an intelligent, constant woman. Her only ambition was for Thomas and his literary career. Cyril must be thinking of W. B. Yeats's wife, Georgie, who helped spark William's poetry with her spirit writing. I would not want to do spirit writing. I would not favor meeting a ghost, and my hand is not driven by shades.

But how odd and interesting to encounter a man in the quiet farm countryside of Wisconsin who knows these things and tries to apply such configurations. This seems to be his art, and he appears to have practiced it all of his life. But now that he grows old, his sources seem to sometimes run together like watercolors. I wonder who he communicated with all his years in this preoccupied, insular dairy country? I suspect he's spent a good deal of time talking to himself. I've never met anyone quite like him.

Yesterday he asked me if I knew who Felix "Doc" Blanchard was. Was he testing my sanity? I had no *idea* who Felix Blanchard was! It seems he was the star fullback for the army military academy football team in the middle 1940s. According to Cyril, he was perhaps the most powerful runner who ever played the game. Cyril knew that he had scored three touchdowns against the navy team in 1946 and had a total of nineteen for the season. His jersey number was 35, and if he ever ran into you, you would go "oof" and never forget number 35.

Cyril was quite adamant that I get all this right, as if he were filling in a great gap in my mind. And yes, I have committed it to memory—and can already feel my life . . . improving. This is far better than hearing someone complain about how their feet hurt. Cyril has an obscure brio which beguiles me.

After our walks, I am worn out by the time we reach my door. But I will take more walks with him. I must figure out a way to return the favor of his constant flow of information. Perhaps I can quiet him down long enough to read him some poetry or show him some pictures or play some music for him, perhaps put some essence behind all those facts he holds in his head about poets, artists, saints, composers, movie stars . . . and old football players, and obscure medieval women, and jazz musicians, and decadent politicians, and opera singers, and . . .

I requested that the staff of the care home help me bring more of my art books from the farm along with a small standing bookcase shelf that would accommodate them. The books make my room warmer, but also smaller.

These little rooms. We try to disguise them in our various ways with our possessions—but they are what they are—holding cells for the doomed. Sometimes we vacate them suddenly, and sometimes we linger a long while in them as we slowly, slowly empty. The staff removes hard-edged or sharp things from our rooms so that we cannot injure ourselves or worse. Things disappear from our minds into the abyss as we sit in these rooms by ourselves—textures are removed, layers are stripped away, our essences are changed and peeled off—leaving strange traces, a sort of melancholy pentimento, until we are down to our true substance, and our final mission: the movement toward the great void.

That is why I will take walks with Cyril and sit with him at meals—because I want to help him hold on to the fascinating things he has put into his head. He is unique, has spent his whole life gathering lives. So many remembered lives— so much better than one lonely death, or a million lost or vacant lives.

CHAPTER 9

Cyril

Every night before I go down to the dining hall to sit with Louise for dinner, I watch the evening news on television for an hour. Louise refers to this as my "evening waltz with death," and I often appear in the hall for dinner looking like an undertaker. It is an old habit, I've done this for years: I watch the news because I'm looking for *lives*—but it is a kind of penance, too, and I don't often find lives that I want to keep.

Here I am, this lucky guy who has lived in these wooded, driftless hills for many years. All I have to do is go out in the morning—winter, summer, spring or fall—and turn my head just slightly in any direction, and see something beautiful. But on the news there are helpless people all over the world stuck in scabby, blasted places, who can't get away and are being chewed up and murdered, millions of them, year after year, their lives pulverized before they can even grow up, cheated and deluded by their leaders, governments, and neighbors, drowned, blown up, shot, raped, buried alive, robbed and forgotten by the cunning idiots they have elected to take care of them, doomed by their poorness, remoteness or religion, they've got no lives to do anything with except try to find ways to exist and maybe find something to eat once a day. They can't go to school or play in their blasted streets. They're afraid to go to the market. They can't go to church to pray because it is forbidden. They can't sit three at their café tables, because it is forbidden for more than two people to be conversing at one time in public.

I could tell you the lives of most of them in one long sentence: They're born, they scramble for water and food every day, they feel more hunger; maybe they are given enough time to produce a child who will also be hungry; finally they are killed, dead and alone, by some bullet or a painful disease, or maybe an explosion vaporizes them, some few relatives mourn and cry out for them, wrap their bodies in dirty cloths, place them in ditches, shovel on dirt, and forget them in a few days. Are these potential scholars, scientists, poets, humanitarians? Lives I would want to collect? Who could say? They are gone forever.

Essentially, this is the news, and these are the lives. The only "notable" lives are bozo dictators and politicians, who dither and blow off, fill their personal coffers, and primp for the crowds. The "good" politicians are so busy hustling for votes, being on the take and staving off the opposition that they completely forget how to be constructive. These are not the kinds of lives I want to remember or keep, but sometimes they seem to be the only lives being lived.

Once or twice a month pictures are broadcast on the news program of the lost young people who've died in our American wars—gone before they have any light in their eyes, down they go into body bags, into the ground as if they'd never existed in this world, mourned only by some remote family and a small group of friends. Why do I watch this without expectation night after night? Perhaps I think it is my duty as an informed citizen. After watching this, it is such a relief to go sit at dinner with Louise, but sometimes I am not very good company.

Louise ignores the news and counts on it for nothing; she has other things on her mind. Louise is a quick study. Right away she sized up this care home and recognized it as nothing more than a staging area for advanced crones and codgers. You can either make the best of this when you come here, or wither away in your own elemental sadness like a stricken elm.

Louise is determined not to start sucking her thumb, and she won't allow me to feel sad or sorry for myself either. I admire her attitude, so I am always anxious to see her when I go down for dinner after my waltz with death, and afterward, if the weather is nice, take an evening constitutional with her around the grassy islands in the parking lot.

But this night I'm a bit late as I step into the dining area and I see there is a man sitting at our table with her. They are in conversation. I back out of the room again, almost falling over someone's wheelchair, and catch my breath.

I recognize this guy. His name is Danderman, and he'd been a couple of years ahead of me in high school all those years ago. He was one of the athletic hotdogs, quarterback on the football team, a jaunty shortstop/pitcher type; later I think he ran some insurance agency in Readstown, became a councilman and school board member. A small town civic leader whose tenth-tier life wasn't worth keeping track of— but there he is in his old age, leaning toward my new friend, Louise, like the world's biggest pooh-bah. And she is listening to him.

My chilblains start itching, my chopped sirloin nose is running. Is this jealousy I'm feeling? I guess so. I consider not going into the dining room. The singer is standing with her fingertips on the table and singing "Twilight Time." She's all over the place with the tune.

Finally I suck it up—Cyril, I say to myself, what kind of a chicken shit are you? Get in there! And so I step back into the dining room, tapping my canes loudly as I walk toward the table where Louise and Danderman are sitting. I would have been clicking my heels, too, but I'd forgotten to change from my slippers.

Louise looks up, happy to see me, and smiles her beautiful smile. "Good evening, Cyril," she says, as she always does. "Have you met Mr. Danderman?"

Danderman gazes at me coldly, not acknowledging the introduction. "You look like you need to sit down," he says to me, and gestures to the chair beside him. But I shuffle around and sit on the other side of Louise.

I don't recall that I've ever exchanged a word with Danderman over the many years we both have lived in this same little area. He's always been too important to acknowledge my existence. I remember that he would occasionally buffalo me aside in the halls of the high school, but he never deigned to speak to me, except perhaps once or twice a jaunty nod and passing "Whadayasay." He always had a bimbo on his arm. Now he measures me carefully. Is he planning to move in on Louise?

Not by the few gray hairs of *my* chinny chin chin!

What has he really done with himself over all this time? Not much after a few years of high school glory—but he'd managed to make those moments last all his life. I was pretty sure that Louise would not be impressed, although I have to admit that Danderman *looks* a hell of a lot better than I do. He's kept most of his hair—I notice he's touched it up with brown coloring—and is only a little puffy around the middle. All I have going for me are my bandages that Louise has painted with small flowers, and my skin that looks like rancid bacon.

Danderman looks a little like Vidkun Quisling, the Norwegian World War II traitor, and I'm about to tell him this when he, in his quick, assertive manner, asks: "You having a good time here?" His eyes are like chilled plastic ice cubes and his mouth is slack. I think right then that I sure as hell am not going to give Danderman a life to identify with—not even Quisling's.

"I'm getting through the days," I answer him. "Nights are a little tricky sometimes."

He's looking at my bandages, my nose, and where my missing ear should be. "What the hell hit you, man—a double Peterbilt?"

"I got mugged by a polar bear," I tell him.

Louise has a pleasant chuckle at this. I can usually make her laugh—and she likes that.

Danderman seems flustered that she thinks my remark is clever. He's a veteran libertine, not used to being one-upped, especially by a corpus delicti. He shifts in his plastic chair and gives me a patronizing smile as he tries to stare me down. I hold his gaze. We sit in silence for a while. Finally Danderman asks, "What have you been doing with yourself since high school?"

"That was a long time ago. I kept to myself. I had jobs in town over the years."

More silence. I gnaw on my rubbery chicken. The singing lady is doing "The Little White Cloud That Cried" now. It's pretty bad.

"Somebody should shoot that old bag," Danderman says.

"She'll die singing," Louise says. "There are worse ways to go. She's determined to entertain us. I think it's very generous of her."

"She ruins my digestion." Danderman grinds in his chair.

I chew another bite of chicken. "What did you do with yourself after high school?" I ask him after a while. "I know you had an insurance agency. You probably played golf."

"Yeah, I was a golfer. Still can hit a few. I played slow-pitch softball until I was in my early fifties." He's looking at Louise like he would like to eat her with a spoon.

"You look a lot like Donkey Thomas," I say suddenly.

Here I go! Now I've done it. I guess I just can't help myself—I'm going to give this pissant a life anyway.

Danderman is surprised and sits up in his chair, looking challenged. "Who was Donkey Thomas?" He puts both of his big hands on the table.

"He was an outfielder/first baseman for a lot of major league teams. Not the Hall of Famer Frank Thomas who played for the White Sox, but he was Frank 'the Donkey' Thomas, a big strong, white guy, mean as hell, he hit double-figure home runs eight times, but he struck out a lot. He pulled the ball and hit some of the longest foul balls in major league history. Strong guy—not the smartest. He had a standing bet with anyone that he could take their hardest throw with his bare hands, so you can imagine what a dope he was. It used to drive his managers crazy, but he'd dare people and never lost the bet; he even took Willie Mays's best shot with his bare hands. And he'd stick his skinny nose in anyone's face. One time the Phillies traded for him, and the first day he got into a fist fight with their star, Dick Allen, and they placed him on waivers the next day."

There—I'd given Danderman a life, despite myself. I'm not sure he liked it, but I enjoyed it. I even elaborated and embroidered the tale now, just for my delectation: "Donkey Thomas played seven years for Pittsburgh, then bounced around with eight other teams in half a dozen years. Managers couldn't stand him—nobody could stand him—so they kept moving him on. The new teams kept hoping he'd at least hit a few home runs and win a game or two for them.

"One of his managers was mad at him one time and commented to sportswriters, 'He needs to change his deodorant.' Donkey Thomas could not be managed, but if they had a little extra room on their roster, they wanted his power. He was all muscle, but the muscle ran into his head as well. You look like him."

Danderman looked as if he'd swallowed a baby alligator. We all sit quietly at the table for a few moments, listening to the singer struggling now through "Ebb Tide." I nibble at my cold peas.

"What really happened to you?" Danderman asks after a while. "You run your electric cart into a display of canned peaches at Walmart, or something?"

"I got abducted by a criminal and he left me out to die in a snowstorm. I was lucky the sheriff found me. What happened to you?" I asked him. I was pretty worked up by now. "You look like you got old, too. Were you surprised? Did you finally get your bare ass snapped with the biggest wet towel in the locker room?"

"Gentlemen," Louise says after some moments of white silence, "please. You must excuse me. I have some things to attend to." She stands, and Danderman and I struggle to our feet.

"I'll walk you to your room," I offer quickly.

"That won't be necessary tonight, Cyril," she says. "You've not finished your meal yet."

"Allow me," Danderman says.

"You sit with Cyril," she tells him. "He's just been in the hospital for a while and doesn't know too many people." She's off with her cane tap-tapping quicker than I've ever seen her move, escaping us both.

Danderman watches her walk away. "Pretty foxy lady," he comments. "Nice legs." He turns to me.

"Listen, junior, you keep trying to show me up like that, you'll be wishing the cops hadn't found you in that blizzard." His demeanor has changed. He's edged forward and is leaning on me like Danderman the tough jock.

"Here now!" I say. "Aren't we a bit old to be talking tough to each other?"

"You started it, Mr. Frosty. What kind of jobs did you have? Cleaning up the toilets at the VFW? I could have hired you to mow my lawns, except you probably wouldn't have got the lines straight."

After all these years Danderman was finally speaking to me. Were the two of us going to have a dustup over a woman right here in the dining room of the old folks' home?

That would probably be a first for this place. I notice there is a crutch propped against his chair. That could be his weapon, and I could use one of my walking sticks. *Satisfaction! En garde!* Clackety-clack.

I'd seen Danderman hobbling painfully around the halls; his crabbed pace was obviously making him irritable. Years ago in high school I saw him run for a seventy-yard touchdown. But now—even I could probably dazzle him with a little footwork despite my missing four toes.

Poor Louise, how disgusting for her! What silly boys she must think we are. I'll pick her some flowers from one of the beds in the parking lot. In the meantime, I have to deal with Danderman, the ex-jock who has his big nose way out of joint.

"Look, it's too bad we're having this little rumpus," I say. "Both of us should probably watch our blood pressures. How about a game of checkers sometime?"

Danderman struggles to his feet. I wonder if he is going to smack me with his crutch—but he tucks it under his armpit. He sticks his big red puss down close to mine; his breath is like air off the town dump. "Listen, snowman, don't butt in next time you see me talking to a woman! It ain't polite."

Suddenly everything seems at stake, my vision flares. I take a blast of air into my lungs, blood rushing to what's left of my fingertips. I snarl back at Danderman: "Up your ass with a ten-foot pole!"

Men are rote creatures. They curse each other like little boys when they don't know what else to do, they revert to teenage playground blurt. I'd never dreamed of saying such a thing to someone like Danderman. In the old days I would have kept my mouth shut, hoping for the best—but age has ground us both down to our nubs, and things have evened out a bit.

Danderman starts to walk away, but when he hears my response he turns and faces me again, drooling with anger. I think—this is it, he's going to come back and deal with my ass. People sitting at nearby tables are alarmed. But then he remembers who we both are and where we are. His eyes flick around the room; he bites it off and jerks around to walk away.

The scene we had created was like a weigh-in at a heavyweight boxing match. I'd occasionally seen men brawling over women in the parking lot at Burkhum's, and always thought that all that blood came too readily. But now I feel like Saint George. If necessary, for the fair Louise, I will face the fetid breath of this half-dead dragon. Bring him on! I'll knock him down on his goddamned keister! I'll drop him like a hot spud!

CHAPTER 10

Louise

We live such small lives in this place. All of us are here because we can no longer stand on our own. I remember my mother writing to me from France, worrying about her coming retirement from her teaching job. "What will I do?" she asked me. I wrote back that she should be free—paint watercolors, keep a memoir, do volunteer work and help others, travel to Italy or Scandinavia or North Africa. She had never been anywhere. But my uncles told me that she retired uneasily and sat small in her house. She lost weight, grew depressed and got even smaller, became so weak she couldn't take care of herself. By the time they moved her to a care facility she was so reduced she died within weeks.

Is it any wonder I resisted the idea of coming here to this rest home? I can already feel myself diminishing. Sleep closes in at all times and from all angles. Should one attempt to be calm and acquiesce to this entombment? We have so little choice. I fall slumbering over my books. My watercolors are runny and frustrating. Music becomes noise. I can only read for a half hour at a time before my eyes grow dim. The television set is a box full of babbling, intrusive idiots. The advertisements attempt to suck my blood.

How can I give myself to any of this? My entire adult life has been silence, but I made myself large within the quietude. I must strive to do the same in this place.

That man Danderman is trying to be friendly, but he is such an incredible bore, and his attention makes Cyril feel threatened. The two of them act like school boys around each other.

I must give Cyril some assurances. I don't want him to feel that our friendship is at risk. I have never met anyone like Cyril—all of his life he has collected other people's lives and his head is teeming with them. Out of his generous heart he attempts to share his studious good fortune with others, but he is generally avoided. Despite this patronization and now his physical afflictions, he remains buoyant and munificent. I hear the lives he recites with gratitude—they are like gifts. But not everyone listens to him. He needs to be a bit more selective, and I will urge this on him. But who else knows such things? He is someone *using* his mind, flourishing like fresh air in this place, and people are generally suspicious of this.

Cyril says I remind him of Christine de Pisan, and he wants to buy me a Leinenkugel at the tavern across the road. The potentiality of this adventure stirs us both as if it were an exotic trip on the Orient Express. The rules in the home are that we are not supposed to leave the grounds on our own, so we will have to do this on the sly, but this is precisely *why* we should have this forbidden adventure—it will challenge us to *do* something, to stay large in our brief lives.

We begin to lay our plans. Friday nights are bingo nights in the home, so everyone will be busy at the games. We decide that we will make an appearance and play a few cards, then fade away from the crowd. Cyril will go out and around the side of the building to prop open one of the emergency exits with a match book late in the afternoon, and we will slip out that evening. Cyril uses two canes and I require one, so arm in arm with this tripod of assistance we will deliberately make our slow way through the parking lot and across the highway to this tavern called Burkhum's.

Cyril says there is country music on Friday nights—not my favorite genre, but Cyril wonders if we might have a dance. Now wouldn't that be wonderful, if we could do it? I am willing to give it a try—a slow number, so we can support each other. I haven't danced in decades and Cyril says he has never danced. He wants to try. He figures it is time for us to take a step or two, and I agree. Perhaps after several Leinenkugels we will attempt it. The people in Burkhum's Tap would probably welcome a spectacle.

Everyone at the home's bingo party is in a good mood after a day of sunshine. In these driftless hills one earns and deserves the pleasures of springtime after the long winter. If you bear up well to the cold and snow, it makes the warm spring weather even more gratifying. There is much pleasant banter as the bingo cards are played. Cyril and I play three cards before, as prearranged, both of us rise separately and move off to the back hallway as if to go to the restroom. No one notices our departure and the nurses are busy at the desk.

We are down the hall and out the exit door into the fresh twilight like violets "that strew the green lap of the new come spring," both of us greatly excited, hobbling skillfully with our canes across the parking lot toward the highway that crosses between the home and Burkhum's Tap. Cyril is cackling triumphantly. I wish I could hold his hand, but we are both occupied with our canes. We stay close to each other as we move along, happy as a couple of teenagers frolicking in the foothills of a lifetime. It has been many years since I've felt this sort of keenness.

We are accomplished old shufflers—so tap, tap, tap—and we are across the road and quickly at the edge of Burkhum's gravel parking lot. There are early crickets in the bushes around the building; we can hear a car door slamming and people laughing. The moon is not quite full, but it is gibbous and high, and there is the sound of a fiddle, a loud guitar, and double bass coming out of the tavern.

CHAPTER 11

Cyril

The last time I was in Burkhum's on a Friday night I got myself into some serious heat, but I can tell already that this evening is going to be better. This is an *occasion*! My first date ever! I've waited a long time, but now I'm out here doing the town with a real knockout. Louise!

The Tap is jumping, but I spot a table for two off in a corner. Louise seems a bit overcome by the crowd and loud music. I tuck one of my canes up under my arm, take her elbow and proudly steer her through. We are the oldest people in Burkham's by at least twenty years. Folks are checking us out and moving their chairs back so we can hobble through like royalty.

Burkhum hires extra waitresses to work on weekend nights—but the man himself personally comes to our table to take our order. I suspect he might be feeling just a tad guilty about what happened to me—as he was the guy who put me out into the storm that Friday night when I got iced, and I haven't seen him since.

"Cyril!" Burkhum says. "I'm glad to see you out and around. You doing okay?"

"Oh, a little bit of this, a little bit of that, Burkham, but I'm making it. Thanks for asking. How's business?"

"We're getting by," he says. "Who's your lady friend?" He's looking at Louise and smiles.

"This is Louise," I proudly tell Burkhum. Then to Louise, "Burkhum is the guy who owns this pile."

Louise has put on small earrings and some makeup. She gives him her nicest smile. The way she's fixed her hair— she's like a beautiful white bird. Lord, she is a sight to my eyes! Louise *glows*. I know Burkhum has seen some women in his day, but I can tell he's impressed.

I am mighty proud to be with her. *Cyril*, I keep reminding myself, *here you are on your first date ever. And you are out with a queen.*

"You from around here?" Burkhum asks Louise. He's looking her up and down.

There may be only 693 people in Soldiers Grove, but folks can live a lifetime as neighbors in these driftless hills and never meet. Louise tells him, "My husband and I had a farm two miles in off Highway J. He died a few years ago. I live in the care home now."

"What'll it be?" Burkhum asks.

I proudly order for both of us. "Bring us two Leinenku-gels, Burkhum, and a bag of barbecue chips."

"This one's on me," he announces.

I make as if I'm falling out of my chair. "Burkhum, from *whence* comes this benevolence? Have you been canonized? I *thought* you were looking a little like Saint Vincent de Paul tonight. Do you know about him? He was patron saint of generosity. There's a statue of him in Saint Peter's Basilica in Rome. One time he gave his whole fortune away to ransom 1,200 Christian slaves in North Africa and saved their lives. He was always raising money and helping the poor."

Burkhum quick steps away with our order before I am able to say more. Louise giggles as she watches him retreat. She places her hand on my sleeve. "Dear Cyril, they don't know what to *do* with you!" she says. "You are a beautiful fountain in the driftless hills. If the world were a right place, they'd put up a statue of *you* in Rome."

Burkhum sends over a waitress to deliver our order. "Boss says this is on us," she announces, placing two unopened beer bottles and bag of chips on the table and hustles away. I manage with a little effort to twist off both bottle caps and place Louise's Leinenkugel in front of her, then somehow I manage to wrangle open the bag of chips.

"Do they give you glasses?" Louise looks around.

"Only if you ask. Let me get one for you." I struggle to rise.

"Sit still, dear man!" Louise grasps my wrist to hold me down. She raises her bottle to her lips for a sip. "This is Leinenkugel, isn't it? You told me it is a Wisconsin elixir— good right out of the bottle."

As we sip our beer we chatter with excitement about our escape from the home.

"I liked it best when we were just outside the door," Louise says. "I haven't had a feeling like that since *renfoncement* from school in France. It was like being out-of-body, making our way over here to the Tap. Bless you, Cyril!"

"It's always fun sneaking out of that place, the feeling you get when you're almost to the door and there's still the danger of one of those desk nurses spotting you. When you're outside and clear, it's like a whole hod of bricks has been taken off your shoulders." I take another pull on my Leinie. Louise is smiling as she reflects on our escape.

A *moment* has come. It seems to me that I should now do something or say something significant, but I don't really know how to tell a woman that I like her. I've never expressed affection to *anyone*, but now I want very much to say something to Louise. So right in the middle of the Friday night Burkhum's Tap crowd, I—Cyril, the abominable snowman— utter to the lady: "You know, I spent my whole life alone. That's a *long* time to be talking to yourself. Being with you is like feeling what Oscar Robertson must have felt, making a fast break to the basket in the last seconds of a tie game. I've never said anything like this to anyone, but I have this feeling like I've never had before. I don't feel so wasted when I'm with you. You make me feel happy."

I spray all that out, and now I'm embarrassed. I'd been planning to say something like this for weeks, but it kept changing on me, and now I've probably left out some parts, but I'm glad I finally got something out, and I hope I got it right enough, because it's the truth. My face feels hot.

Louise puts her hands over my gnarled digits and says, "Thank you, Cyril." She looks out over the boisterous crowd, "I remember going to Paris for visits when I was a girl. Of course it dazzled me, but it couldn't have been more exciting than Soldiers Grove is right now with you. Don't blush, dear man. I'm happy to be with you. Let's order another Leinenkugel so we can toast this moment. Do you suppose we could try a dance?"

I am flying again. A dance? With Louise. Oh my God! I've never danced in my life, but I want to hold Louise in my arms and take some steps. I'm going to give it my best shot!

The band has been playing mostly rockabilly, working the dancers hard. Some of those couples are really young and gymnastic, flying around the floor. Louise and I can't afford to get knocked down. But we notice the band plays a slower number once in a while to rest the dancers, so we decide that one of these slow numbers will be the safest time for us to be out on the floor.

"How can we dance with canes?" I ask Louise.

She is scheming. "We'll make them part of our dance. We have to use them to make our way to the floor anyway. We can make it short and easy. It will be fun, Cyril. Don't worry. At first we can just stand in front of each other and sway to the right and left while we lean on our canes, then we can each turn all the way around twice while we have our canes planted on the floor, and come back to the front and sway a few more times. Then we can tuck the canes up under our left arms, take hold of each other with our right arms and make some turns together. Slowly. Remember to stay with the rhythm. That's important. Maybe we can finish by stepping apart at the end, take a bow to each other. Short and sweet, but we will have *done* it. And it will be enough."

"What a plan!" I say. "Diaghilev! Very classy. The cane dance."

"We don't want to fall on our faces out there. We're just going to make a quiet statement, but we want to get it right."

"How about another Leinenkugel?" I suggest.

"Perhaps we should just hold off and have a celebratory round after our dance," Louise suggests.

The band is still bouncing the dancers around, so I excuse myself and go to the men's room. I am nervous. When I shuffle back to our table the band is just starting a slow country waltz, so the dance floor is clearing as people return to their tables for a rest.

"Our time," Louise announces. We are both just a little shaky, but we've made a good plan. I take her hand and help her up from her chair.

Cyril, I say to myself, *this is it. You are on, boy! You are going to dance with the queen in front of everybody.* If I've ever had an *event* in my life—this is it! I'm glad I made it to the men's room. Tentatively we tap our way through the tables to the abandoned dance floor. There is a lull in the conversation as people begin to notice us.

"Let's do it right," Louise whispers. "We are *not* old fools!"

We stand on the dance floor facing each other, sway to the right and to the left as we lean on our canes, then turn slowly around them several times as we have planned. When we face each other again we tuck our canes up under an arm and move to take hold of each other.

This is such a delicious moment, I have been looking forward to it, to have Louise in my arms and be against her! I can feel her back moving, her arms holding me. We lean to each other and circle a few times, the band mercifully slows their tempo just a bit more. People are watching us do our steps and, I think to myself, *the two of us, we are shimmering!*

We finish and step back, tap our canes once, and bow to each other. We are done. We have *danced*. The Tap's patrons are on their feet applauding us. Burkham is behind his bar, beaming and beating his hands together. There are a few cries of encore, more, more, but we are both weary now. We return to our table amidst the ovation. Louise is glistening and smiling. I have held that beautiful lady in my arms!

I have never felt like this in my life. The waitress arrives at our table with a tray full of Leinenkugels. Everyone is buying us rounds. But our evening is almost over.

In a short while we accept someone's offer for a ride back to the home. We walk in the entrance and the night clerk looks up in surprise as we hasten past. When we arrive at Louise's door, she turns, gives me another of her smiles, places her hand on my shoulder, and leans over to give me a kiss on the cheek. "Thank you, Cyril, I've had a wonderful evening," and is gone.

The lights in the hallway grow dim as I struggle for breath, then they brighten and I almost collapse. I hang on and do a sort of prancing shuffle on my canes as I move back to my room. I say to myself: *Cyril, you libertine, you've arrived at last! You have had one hell of a date! You are starting out late, but on top!*

Years ago, when I was a kid, I bought a big remaindered copy of Shakespeare's works at the bookstore in Viroqua. I spent months that summer, making my way slowly through the plays, taking a break from the brief lives and hiding from my plastered parents.

Shakespeare was tough sledding for me some of the time. But I could see, the man liked brief lives, too. I memorized whole passages as I read. It was a great summer by the standards of my youth. Most of those lines have slipped from my memory over the years, but I do remember something Bottom the Weaver said in *A Midsummer Night's Dream*, after his magical night with Titania. He's more than a little confused and dazzled, but he says: "The eye of man hath not heard, the ear of man hath not seen, man's hand is not able to taste, his tongue to conceive, nor his heart to report what my dream was."

He'd had his dream moment, odd Bottom. Now, odd Cyril, you are having yours.

CHAPTER 12

Louise

The escape to Burkhum's Tap has pried open our eyes. Now we envision nothing but further adventures together. We cannot abandon our canes—but there is more brio in our steps now. Our visions extend beyond this home, and we begin to scheme.

A minibus comes to the home twice a week to take residents to Walmart and Walgreens in Viroqua. Sometimes it makes day trips to local park sites and historical attractions, but Cyril and I are bored by these group trips. We have tasted real freedom and now we seek a further range. The excitement of escape is a large part of our experiences.

Today I awakened from a nap and had a vision. Why hadn't I thought of this before? The old Dodge Ram truck that sits idle on my farm! It is still vigorous, I am sure. Heath loved that truck, took wonderful care of it, using it for many of his chores. I used to drive it to town for groceries and other shopping. Why should this wonderful vehicle waste away in the shed near our house, when it could become Cyril's and my chariot? I believe Heath would be pleased for me if he knew this.

In the book of regulations for the home it says we are not allowed to have vehicles on the premises, but who would notice one more blue Dodge truck amongst all the pickups parked around this place every day? The trick will be to manage sneaking it onto the parking lot without being noticed.

The farm is too far away for Cyril and me to make a hike on our canes and fetch it, so I will have to figure a way to get the truck and bring it back to the home without being noticed.

I've rented a few of our farm fields to a dour neighbor and he does necessary chores about the place, and checks the house for me occasionally. I could ask him to bring the truck in for me, but he is such a straitlaced, proper Lutheran I could never persuade him to help me break the rules of the home.

That man, Danderman. He lives in the independent living section of the home and has a car. He's already asked me several times to go out to dinner with him. He could drive me afterward to the farm to pick up the truck. But Cyril dislikes the man intensely. Still, if Danderman could be used to help us accomplish our mission, it would open our lives to greater adventures.

The next time Danderman asks me to dinner I will accept his invitation. Cyril will be beside himself when I tell him—but what is a poor girl supposed to do? Something needs to be done.

Cyril's face grows crimson when I tell him my plan. "I don't want that guy getting romantic with you!" I begin to realize that probably my dear, new friend has never experienced jealousy. He is obviously surprised by how he feels. Despite my reassurances, he pouts like a little boy and looks away.

"Can't we think of another way to get this done?" he insists. "That guy thinks he's Artie Shaw or something. If he *touches* you, Louise, I swear I'll brain him with one of my shillelaghs!"

But everything works out okay. I smile at Danderman the next time I see him in the dining hall, and he does not hesitate to invite me out. At dinner I work hard at boring him to distraction with my talk about art and music. He is more than ready to be rid of me by the time our desserts come. As he finishes his apple pie, I ask him to drop me off at my farm, claiming that I'm going to have an overnight to do some cleaning chores.

He looks at me slyly for a moment. *What on earth*, I think? Then I realize—this man is so preposterously vain, he believes I am hinting at a tête-à-tête! The bumptiousness of him! But then I tell him quite stridently in the restaurant that when I was in France I lived in Paris and posed as a female impersonator. I say it loud enough so that people at surrounding tables turn to gawk at us.

Danderman looks as if he's swallowed a stingray. The waitress brings the bill and I loudly insist upon paying my half. Danderman drives me to my farm and almost pushes me out of his car.

The blue Dodge starts right up in its shed and has a full tank of gas. I turn the motor off while I check things out on the farm, coping with old memories. All of this bears overwhelming sadness, but I don't believe Heath would begrudge me my enjoyment of these last experiences.

Sadly I finger my books and records, putting a few more things in a box to take back with me, waiting until dark to drive the truck into Soldiers Grove, and parking it in a far corner of the home lot.

I find Cyril waiting in the lobby when I slip in the door. But the poor dear has drifted off to sleep in a big green lounge chair. I gently awaken him and immediately he begins to fret about Danderman. I buy him a carton of chocolate milk from one of the vending machines and talk quietly with him until he is able to calm down.

"That creep thinks he's Lothario!" Cyril fusses. "He didn't try anything, did he?"

"He never got one of his nasty paws on me," I assure Cyril. "I overpowered him with chatter. He couldn't wait to be rid of me."

I pat Cyril's gnarled hand.

I'm very excited about what I accomplished tonight. "Now we have a chariot, my hero," I announce to Cyril. "Who knows what fabulous mysteries lie ahead for us? We can dance our dances in La Crosse. Prairie du Chien? Milwaukee? Fond du Lac? Viroqua? Richland Center, Madison? Mineral Point? Do we dare think beyond Wisconsin? Des Moines? Iowa City? Minneapolis? Dubuque? Chicago? San Francisco? The world has suddenly yawned open to us!"

I am soaring and my dreams are large enough to frighten Cyril. But I have been *at home* all my life. Now I want to roam, to *do* some things. "We could drive to Chicago airport and take the overnight flight from Chicago to Paris," I suggest. Cyril looks as if he might slip out of his chair onto the floor. I realize I am frightening him.

"But dear Cyril, my heart leaps up!" I tell him. "The road has opened. It beckons to us. The world is *ours* to see now, and possibilities are endless."

"Maybe we should start slowly," Cyril says cautiously. "If they throw us both out of this home, we'll be lost like Hansel and Gretel wandering in the driftless hills. Where would we go? They'd find us wandering the streets some day, looking for cardboard to sleep under. Can't we just start with a quiet picnic along the Kickapoo? Or a pork cutlet in Readstown? There's a nice hotel bar in Boscobel. I'll buy you a strawberry margarita."

"That's all very exciting," I say. "Let's start a list. But let's allow ourselves to dream big, too. After some practice, we'll take a few larger chances. Do we dare an overnight someplace? It would have to be done cannily, but we cannot waste this opportunity."

Cyril is still stewing about Danderman. He's thrashing in his green chair. "I just thought of who Danderman looks like," he says: "Charles Laughton after he'd eaten fifty escargots and drunk a quart of brandy. I'm going to punch that man in the stomach and make him explode!"

Boys will be such silly boys. Cyril is cleverer than most, but he is still a boy. It has been a long day and I am weary. I quote to him from Mother Goose:

> *The man in the moon looked*
> *Out of the moon*
> *Looked out of the moon*
> *And said,*
> *'Tis time for all children*
> *On the earth*
> *To think about going to bed.*

CHAPTER 13

Cyril

We've got to plan these early escapes carefully or we'll blow our cover before we even get started. I'm a little worried, now that we've got wheels. Louise is acting like a sprung prisoner; she's got huge ideas and wants to go everywhere at once. I've got the bug, too—but nice and easy, I urge her, cool and measured, that's the only way. A little bit now, a little bit later—and timing is so important. Neither of us has ever traveled beyond Viroqua or Richland Center or Prairie du Chien in our adult lives. We need to practice.

But Louise's restlessness is infectious, so it's up to me to keep a lid on things. She was born in France, grew up there, sailed across the ocean, had a few adventures. I've always just looked at maps and dreamed about all the roads out there! I start itching even more than usual when I look at them now that we've got wheels; I place my finger down on a big map of the United States and run it around: Zanesville, Vacaville, Jasper, Valdosta, Vero Beach, Great Falls, Owensboro, Andalusia, Sag Harbor, Gallup, Queen City, Bangor, Cartersville, Pine Knob, Yonkers, Saginaw, Ruidoso, Opelousas, Mingo Junction, Slippery Rock, Glenwood Springs, Missoula, Knoxville, Chico, Wichita, Decorah, Boone, Roanoke, Scio. I want to go to all of them.

Louise has even bigger eyes—New York, Pittsburgh, Saint Louis, Chicago, Seattle, San Francisco, New Orleans,

Savannah. Lord . . . even Paris, London! That's the way she thinks.

Now I'm starting to think like Jack Kerouac. And Louise is much prettier than Neal Cassady. Let's go!

Take it easy, Cyril! Cool it. Work your way out gradually. You'll get to the moon yet, solve all the mysteries, touch all the places, just don't get lost on the way or you'll end up walking down some snowy highway again, peeing your pants and freezing your balls off.

So I try to rein Louise in a little bit, too. It is wonderful to see her so excited, she is so beautiful when her cheeks get red—but I try to make her focus a bit more locally, at least at first. Morning excursions would probably be best to start, maybe once in a while extending one of our capers through the lunch hour—so long as we don't do it so often that staff will start to take notice.

We've both signed contracts with the home, agreeing to their rules and restrictions. They have their own responsibilities, and government regulations they must follow. If they discover us breaking rules all the time, we could be expelled like truant school kids. We must take care.

Afternoons probably would not be so good. Old folks get sleepy in the afternoons. We need our naps. So it is mornings probably to slip out, and evenings—once in a while maybe we can dress up and sneak out for a fancy date night.

We begin with something elemental. I still have one of my old fishing rods in my room, and we discover a nice spinning rod and reel that Heath had kept behind the seat of the blue Dodge.

One morning we slip out through the parking lot to the truck, giggling like a couple of kids playing hooky. With tremendous excitement—and just a little guilt and nervousness—we drive slowly out of the lot, stop at a bait shop a short way out of town and buy night crawlers and shiners, then for our lunch I buy cheese curds, peanut butter, crackers, and a quart of orange pop and plastic glasses at the Mobil Quick Stop before we buzz off to a fishing spot I know along the Kickapoo River. The water is slow, and so is the fishing at first, only an occasional nibble. We don't mind; it's a sweet day. I find two fold-up chairs in the bed of the Dodge and set them up on the riverbank so we can sit while we're fishing. Louise baits her own hook.

"Hemingway thought fishing was immortal activity," I philosophize to Louise as I pull my bobber out of the water and cast it into a more likely place. "Here we are, like two gods. You know—you don't grow older during the time you're fishing. And you have to *believe* in the future. That's what fishing is all about. In a few minutes I'm going to hook into a trout," I assure Louise. "I'll cook it over some burning sticks for our lunch."

I think some more about Hemingway. How he was restless and acted tough. "Ernest thought that if you can bring yourself to hit a man hard in the face, you will win a fight," I tell Louise. "I've never had a fist fight, but I'm going to smack Danderman's nose if he comes sniffing around you again."

Louise looks annoyed, but I go on boasting, "I'm going to bust him a good one." But then I begin to think about my cramped up old hands and how much they would hurt if I hit something hard with them. Then about how my poor nose would probably come completely unglued if someone punched it.

I chatter some more, but change my tune a little, "Maybe I'll just dazzle Danderman with footwork; he'll never get a glove on me. I'll be like Billy Conn the first time he fought Joe Louis." But then I remember—I'm an old guy walking with two canes. "Well, I'll give him a whack up the side of his head with one of my sticks. I'll give him a head butt." Ouch . . .

I get worked up when I think about Danderman, and it is a very strange feeling. "I'll smack him so he won't forget!"

I am breathing hard, like Beowulf boasting about what he's going to do when Grendel comes. I've never felt this way before. I want to damage Danderman.

"Silly boy," Louise says. "Cyril, will you calm yourself, please! Remember, he helped us get the blue Dodge. You're going to have a heart attack. Watch your bobber."

But I go on stewing.

"Cyril," Louise says at last, "you are my dearest and only friend. That man is of absolutely no interest to me. You are not challenged. You don't have to bash him. I don't want you to get hurt. It's a beautiful day. Unwind yourself. If the fish know you're agitated, they won't bite."

We sit quietly again, and eventually catch a few small bream. We are excited when the bobbers go down, but throw the fish back. By the time Louise starts driving us back to the home we are both weary.

Being jealous is hard work. I am finding this out. It just plain peters you out.

We slip back into the home like guilty lovers in the early afternoon, but no one even looks at us. It's almost disappointing.

We wait a few more days before planning our next adventure. Louise wants to go to the bookstore in Viroqua. One morning we slip out of the parking lot in the blue Dodge shortly after breakfast while the home staff is busy cleaning up after the meal. It is so much fun to be screwing off. The day is overcast, but cool and pleasant as Louise drives the county highway over to Viroqua.

Three very literate, efficient women have run the bookstore for years. They are delighted to see Louise. She'd been one of their very good customers, always stopped in the store to browse and buy books when she was grocery shopping in Viroqua, but she hasn't been here since the death of her husband.

Louise has recently read a review of a new biography of the Brontë sisters. She wants to buy the book. As we were driving to Viroqua I gave her my brief lives of the Brontës—one at a time—Anne, Emily and Charlotte, their sad, amazing, strange existence on the moors, and I even added a little about crazy Branwell, their brother. I've got all the Brontës down pretty good. They are a tricky bunch.

"Now you won't have to buy the book," I tease Louise when I finish my recitation, but Louise has purchased books all her life; she has a lot of them, and she reads them. She is ready to put her money down for the book. I used to stop occasionally in the Viroqua bookstore, too, before I met Louise. I'd even buy a book once in a while, too, but mostly I just read stuff off the shelves, trying to keep myself up to date on lives. The bookstore ladies were always very kind about this, but sometimes they would shame me into paying for a book. The three of them seem delighted and very surprised to see Louise and me together.

The biography of the Brontës that Louise wants to buy is a big book, a 450 pager, a hardback that costs forty bucks. "What are you going to do?" I ask Louise. "Sell your farm to buy that?" But Louise peels out two twenties from her purse without even gazing at me.

I must be looking particularly cadaverous this morning because the book ladies are peering strangely at me. Funny thing about getting old: some days you feel okay—and once in a while, just for a few minutes, even a little bit good—but then you catch a look in a mirror and realize that you look like you've been going to school with a bunch of piranha. It is best not to reflect on yourself too often.

"Cyril, have you been all right?" one of them finally asks.

"Never better," I tell her. And I meant it.

I'm sure the Brontës have heard about my ordeal. The newspapers picked up on my story and wire services ran it across the country. People are always fascinated by stories of peril, and they seem particularly to like it when someone is able to trick death. There was coverage on some of the prime time news shows, long stories about my ordeal, some "portraits" and other shortened squibs. The home nurses actually started a scrapbook of them. Not too many old guys walk out of the freezer alive. For about a quarter of an hour I was the most famous citizen of Soldiers Grove.

The Brontës are still looking at me. I say finally, "Well, I'm not feeling too bad. A little kink here and there, but I think I'm good for some more time. Sorry I forgot to comb my hair."

They don't laugh. They look serious. I must be looking really hammered this morning.

"He's doing just fine," Louise finally assures them, as she thumbs through her big new book. "Don't pay any attention to how he looks."

"We were really happy to hear you got the big bravery award," one of them says. "Now maybe you can pay for a book once in a while." They all giggle.

These women have always enjoyed giving me nudges, and I always try to give them back as good as I get: "Don't get carried away," I warn them. "Reading is hard for me these days. Half an hour of it and my eyeballs feel like two gritty mibs at the end of recess. I can barely read the directions on my corn flakes box. Besides, I cashed in that check and put all the money in an old sock. I only kept out enough for chocolate milk and a few Leinenkugels for Louise. Not a penny for books. Now I can't even remember where I put the sock. That's the way it goes with old guys like me."

I notice that the jacket illustration of the new biography of the Brontë sisters uses the portrait painted by their brother, Branwell. At first Branwell had placed himself in the middle of the picture between Emily and Charlotte, but later someone—probably Branwell himself—decided to paint out his own image so that there seems to be a ghost beween Emily and Charlotte, and then the picture was roughly folded up and put aside somewhere.

As the three bookstore ladies stand together watching us, I gently take the big book from Louise's hand and hold it up so she can compare the cover illustration to the three women standing in front of us. "See. There they are," I say to Louise, "Anne, Charlotte, and Emily. It's uncanny!" The resemblance *is* remarkable.

Louise takes hold of the book, looking back and forth between it and the bookstore women. She nods and giggles. "Yes, it's perfect."

I've always tried to figure out those bookstore women. Now I know they are the Brontë sisters come from the moors of northern England to the driftless hills of Wisconsin to sell books. How lucky we are they came to Viroqua!

I tell them, "We will never refer to you as anyone else. Just look at them, Louise! The Brontë sisters. I can't even remember your real names anymore. From this moment on you are Anne, Emily, and Charlotte," I tell them.

Balaclava

Balaclava is sitting on a toilet in a locked filthy stall in the men's room of a convenience store just off an Indiana highway. As he strains, he skims his eyeballs over a dusty copy of an area newspaper called the Terre Haute Clarion that he'd found in a waste stack in the hallway just outside the restroom. Now he notices that the issue is months old, and he is ready to wad the stupid, goddamned thing up and pitch it over into the next stall.

Two nights before, Balaclava had almost been fried by the Hoosiers and he's still shaky about it. He'd been working his way across the state, zigzagging around, sometimes sleeping in the truck, hiding it out of sight when he robbed stores on the edges of little towns. Quick, easy stick-ups— mostly terrified teenage clerks who put their hands up fast and shoveled out the cash when he showed them his big cannon.

If the clerk was a guy, when he had the money he'd give him a rap on his noggin, just enough to stun him, then hustle out and drive the Dodge away before they could come to their senses to see what he was driving. If it was a woman, he'd shove her hard in the face and push her down, warning her not to look before he ran away. He was adding assault to his robbery when he conked the

~ 113 ~

clerks—but to hell with it! His hole was already plenty deep.

But he was growing bored with this penny-ante stuff. What he scored was barely enough to pay for his gas, beef jerky, beer and chips. He needed something big.

A couple of nights before he'd been poking around in a Kwik 'n' Ezy near Wabash, waiting for some Mars bars grade schoolers to clear out so he could make his heist and get on down the road. Finally, after a lot of petering around, the baby yokels departed. Balaclava was just getting ready to bring out his artillery, when a local police car pulled right up outside the door and two paunchy cops walked in.

He was breathing hard, thought he was going to bite it right then, but the cops walked past him and helped themselves to bags of peanuts from the counter, and started talking with the clerk—a big kid with one hell of a build, probably an ex-local football star.

Everything was very yakkety yak and local. Balaclava has never been easy in the same room with authorities, and he doesn't like small talk. It was time to move his ass out of there—so he was heading for the door when the big ex-jock boy clerk looked up over the cops' shoulders and said loudly, "Hey, buddy! You want something?"

The cops turned to look at Balaclava. The fucking kid was just showing off for the bulls—but now all eyes were on him.

And yes, Balaclava is something to see—huge in his ugliness, fierce in his black mackinaw and strange hat snapped up on its sides. "Naw, I'm fine," he said, "just lookin' around." He kept on moving toward the door.

"Hold on a minute, friend," one of the cops said, and came over to stand in front of him. "You from around here?"

"Just passing through."

The patrolman was looking him over carefully. Balaclava doesn't hold up well when the fuzz are close up on him. He doesn't like the smell of them. He's had his bellyful of blue boys. He tried to look steady at the guy, but couldn't mask his distaste. Were they thinking about putting a move on him? He couldn't quick draw the big gun on his ankle, but he had his hand on the cook's small pistol in his coat pocket, and it was cocked and loaded. He figured he could probably drop both of them before they got to their holsters.

The cop looked him up and down. "You planning to stick around here for a while?" he asked Balaclava.

"Naw, like I say, I'm just passing through. I've got to get to Peoria tonight."

"That's a haul," the cop said. "You better get going." He didn't ask to see Balaclava's driver's license, but he eyeballed him carefully and Balaclava held the man's gaze. The cop decided that Balaclava was probably going to be more trouble than he was worth.

"Better roll, mister!" the cop said. "It's a long way to Peoria." And Balaclava did it. It bugged his ass to just trot out of that place like some teenie weenie, but he got the hell out of there.

God, he hates it when he's got to skedaddle like that with his tail between his legs! He thought about coming back later and getting a piece of that show-off kid. He could have made him look like chopped beets. But he kept on going. He didn't need to invite more trouble.

When he'd pulled the truck from around the corner of the convenience store the cop was standing outside, watching him drive away. Balaclava was glad he'd hammered the license plate up under the bumper. He watched in his rear view mirror, but the bull didn't turn on his flashers and come after him.

Why do these sons of bitches have to dog him? He cut off the highway onto a side road and drove until he came *to another larger road, turned onto this and drove until he came to a huge shopping mall parking lot. He pulled into a back row, selected a big red Ford hombre truck, checking to make sure it didn't have an alarm system, then cross-wired it, and quickly switched license plates with the other vehicle.*

Now he is sitting in the filthy men's room stall. He tosses the outdated Terre Haute newspaper on the floor. Fucking podunk Indiana! He is reaching for the toilet paper dispenser when a small headline in the paper catches his eye: WISCONSIN SENIOR CITIZEN RECEIVES NATIONAL AWARD FOR BRAVERY. He takes up the paper again. The story is a very brief wire service clip:

> *"NEW YORK (AP)—An elderly man from Soldiers Grove, Wisconsin, Cyril Solverson, has been named the winner of the Award for Courage from The American Valor Society. The $50,000 award, presented at a black tie ceremony at the Waldorf Astoria in New York on December 17, is only the third such annual award given by the distinguished society.*

> *"Mr. Solverson, still recovering from injuries suffered when he was assaulted and abandoned for dead in a blizzard by a robber, was unable to attend the ceremonies in person. The award was accepted in his name from the society by Mayor Bloomberg, who, in his remarks, marveled at how an older man could struggle four miles after being assaulted, through a raging snowstorm to almost reach his destination.*

> *" 'Thank God he was found,' the mayor commented. 'We have a tendency in our great city to*

think that the only real stories come from New York, but they come from Soldiers Grove, Wisconsin, too, and I am proud to accept in Mr. Solverson's honor, this award for his amazing tale of courage which took place in a remote region of the heartland of our country.'

"The $50,000 prize award money has been forwarded to Mr. Solverson, who is still being treated in a hospital in Wisconsin."

The toilet paper dispenser is empty. Balaclava curses broadly; suddenly roaring with fury, he batters the side of the metal partition with both his heavy fists. He hears the guy who had been using the urinal next to his stall hustle out of the restroom in midstream without washing his hands.

Balaclava rages and hammers some more, making tremendous thunder, feeling as if he is about to explode: "I never assaulted that mangy fucker!" he shakes his hairy head back and forth. "I let him go!" he is snarling. "Now they make him a hero and give him the whole bank!"

He smashes on the partition some more, shouting, "Fifty thousand bucks! For bravery! Is there an award for mercy? I gave him mercy! That old fucker was peeing his pants and I let him go. Now I'm sleeping in my truck, stealing beef jerky and Twinkies, and that fossil is high on the hog!"

Balaclava booms his fury still more, quivering and groaning with rage, hammering the graffiti in the stall. Eventually he manages to use a crumpled piece of the Terre Haute Clarion *to wipe himself.*

He roars out of the parking lot, laying dark rubber out onto the highway, but then he clamps down on his temper, sets the cruise control to sixty-five, and drives with steady purpose through the night. Sitting on his rage, but keeping his speed legal, he presses steadily out of Indiana into Illinois, past Peoria, on his way to Soldiers Grove.

Chapter 14

Louise

Cyril and I are having many exciting escapades away from the home now, and are becoming almost careless. I sometimes feel that the staff people are purposely ignoring us, just looking the other way as we make our furtive exits. Sometimes we slip back into the home well after the dinner hour and no one questions us. The people at the desk seem almost bemused when they see us, as if they know that something is going on. Oh those *two*!

I have taken to leaving an occasional nice tip under my plate after I've dined in the hall, and sometimes I leave an envelope out for the people who do the cleaning.

I've heard that someone is always paying in America. It is the way things work, the way things get done—or not done. Little envelopes or massive secret electronic transfers buying favors or silence or service or protection. The whole nation is on the take. I don't tell Cyril about my tipping because it would only make him fret.

By now we've snuck out to most of the reasonable local escape possibilities: decent bars, the few acceptable restaurants, fishing spots, historic sites, antique stores, and often the bookstore in Viroqua to see the Brontë sisters.

Cyril seems to have become more comfortable with the idea of ranging out a bit farther. Perhaps now I can persuade him to dare an overnight somewhere.

Madison is a two-hour drive away. Years ago I went there several times with Heath for appointments at the Department of Natural Resources, but this was during the Vietnam time; the town seemed tense then, almost explosive. The war was horrible, and activists were on the streets daily making quiet statements that frequently turned into loud demonstrations. Heath was an army veteran, but we sometimes joined the protests when we were through with our appointments in Madison. Occasionally as a special treat we'd stay overnight.

I recall a pleasant hotel situated by one of the three lakes. I talk to Cyril about it and, after we have planned carefully, I take the plunge and call the hotel to make reservations for a double room. It is a big chance, but an exhilarating way to further test our capabilities. The drive to Madison takes a little longer than two hours, but to us aged, uncertain travelers it seems like a trip to Tierra del Fuego.

We stop a few times on the way to take bathroom breaks, and at a rest stop to eat our light lunch at a picnic table. When we arrive on the edge of Madison, Cyril uses an old street map to guide us in. He'd found it in the home lounge, unfolds it now and holds it high to give directions like a ship captain to his helmsman. We are both tremendously excited and a little nervous. Cyril gapes in rigid wonder at the large civic and university buildings and Wisconsin capitol dome. He's never seen anything like this.

After we check into our room at the hotel, we take a much needed nap, each of us using one of the two double beds. The room is large and the staff has placed a lovely bouquet of flowers on the bureau for us and a complimentary bottle of fizzy wine with two glasses, apparently thinking when they took our reservation on the phone that we were young lovers on a weekend *tête-à-tête*. *C'est la vérité*. We shall see, we will.

Later we have tea in the hotel bar before tottering out onto the streets. Along State Street there is a long row of shops, bars, galleries, restaurants. Cyril is fascinated with these establishments. He has never seen such an accumulation of special commerce and is overwhelmed by the crowded sidewalks. Everyone is considerate, making way as we shamble along with our canes.

It is a warm day and eventually we stop at an outdoor café to share a draft beer and some pretzels. We watch the passing of young people, professors, politicians, students, even a few common citizens, some almost as old as we are.

We walk on, and as we turn one corner there is a large, secondhand bookshop. Cyril is enchanted, becoming lost in its caverns, the section of biographies and autobiographies almost sweeping him away.

As Cyril browses I chat with the owner, a pleasant man who seems more like a keeper of catacombs than a shopkeeper. He tells me that business is sharply down, that he has had to dismiss most of his staff. His only recourse is to mine the Internet for specialized customers, so he spends most of his days on the computer—instead of like the old days when he sat at his cash register, discussing books with customers, happily watching them roam his shelves and depart with armloads of venerable volumes. He is elated to witness our excitement as we plug through his stacks.

Finally I manage to draw Cyril out of the musty shadows of the biography section. I purchase a few rare British mysteries, and Cyril has found old books on Saint Thomas Aquinas, John Clare and—most precious of all—an antique leatherbound volume called *A Universal Biographical Dictionary*, published in New York in 1795, subtitled *The Lives of the Most Celebrated Characters of Every Age and Nation*, with a description under the title, "Embracing Warriors, Heroes, Poets, Philosophers, Statesmen, Lawyers, Physicians, Divines,

Discoverers, Inventors, and Generally All Such Individuals, as From the Earliest Periods of History to the Present Time, Have Been Distinguished Among Mankind," hand inscribed in now browned floral cursive by "Arnold Aldrich of Smithfield, R.I. 1795. $1.75." Beneath this inscription Mr. Aldrich or someone has drawn in wide ink a swirling tornado figure with five diminishing curls descending halfway down the page; inside of each swirl are notches that look like quotation marks. The "storm" curls down to land between two prominent dots which are placed above what looks like a paved, striped highway—something that did not exist in those early days. The book was later presented—as noted in fading pencil—to "N. D. Aldrich by his mother," probably Aldrich's child or grandchild.

Cyril is consumed by this book, has never realized that such a venerable, mysterious thing might exist in this world. It astonishes him to hold this precious object in his hand. The dealer is asking fifty dollars for the volume. Cyril paces and looks stricken when he hears this. The dealer comes down to forty dollars. Cyril, who is able to look very troubled and alarmingly feeble, continues his slow pacing. The dealer takes pity, makes a "last adjustment": thirty-eight dollars. I am astonished and delighted to watch Cyril go to his wallet and reluctantly peel out the cash.

Since Cyril uses his two canes and I use mine, toting these books will be a problem. The bookstore owner offers to have the books delivered to our hotel by a student helper. We toddle back to the hotel, making several rest stops along the way and by the time we arrive, the books have been delivered to the front desk. We retire exhausted to our room and ease ourselves down on the beds to look through our new treasures, Cyril reverently poring over his antique autobiographical book as if he is holding a copy of the *First Folio*.

He has the book right up against his nose as he reads and squints at the tiny eighteenth century text. Occasionally he flips back to the beginning of the book to look at the signature and strange swirling symbol drawn beneath it. Cyril decides it is a tornado with hail in it, coming down between two stones onto a path. "Maybe it is a sign of Aldrich's power? Or is some terrible memory of weather? It's a storm of good luck for me."

Cyril studies some more. "I think it is more a symbol of his mentality whirling down onto the land. Maybe Aldrich was an old-time guy who collected lives in the eighteenth century. That's more than 200 years ago. He was a pioneer life collector—a guy who came down like a tornado onto the earth to gather brief lives. My ancestor! Maybe my great, great, great, great grandfather? I *need* a relative!"

"Look!" Cyril points to one of the entries on page ninety-seven: " 'BURCKHARDT, John Lewis, native of Lausanne, celebrated as a traveler in Africa, under the patronage of the African Association of London.' Look at this one on page 331: 'PAOLI, Hyacinth, a native of Corsica, who, in 1735, possessed great influence amongst his countrymen as a chief magistrate.'

"What a treasure trove! It's going to take me the rest of my life to get all this mini type into my head. Look at this! 'SHENSTONE, William, an eminent English elegiac and pastoral poet, and a miscellaneous writer, died in 1763, aged 49.' "

It requires all of my bifocaled power to make out just a few words of the tiny eighteenth century printed text, but Cyril is seriously bearing down on this diminutive printing with his worn eyes. He will do anything to collect his lives!

"I'll need my magnifying glass when we get home," he says. Eventually his excitement and eye strain begin to fatigue him and the old book begins to slip from his fingers. I take it from his hands and cover him with a blanket; we nap on the two double beds until it is time to go out for dinner.

We've made an early reservation at a nearby restaurant— one that offers something beyond hamburgers, cheese curds, and fish sandwiches. We take a long time to determine our orders. The menu is French and the prices terrify Cyril. He is ready to walk out, but I persuade him that, because the menu is French and has sentiment for me, he must permit me to treat him. He agrees, but *only* if I permit him to pay for our next meal. Cyril the perfect American!

I finally decide on *reaux de veau,* which Americans call sweetbreads, and a starter of fresh oysters. I help Cyril with the menu and he decides on a starter of *vichyssoise* and an entrée of *tournedos Rossini*, which I explain to him is a fillet steak with Madeira sauce—and some other things. We order a bottle of the house red wine. Cyril is fascinated, relishing his food, and we almost finish the bottle. We conclude with a chocolate mousse and decline coffee. Cyril is a very happy, well-stuffed, slightly intoxicated old man by the time we finish. He has at last relaxed. He is so happy, "I wish I had been born in France, too," he says wistfully as we shuffle slowly back down the street to the hotel, retire to our room, and prepare for bed.

I have brought along one of the pretty nightgowns that I used to wear occasionally on weekends when Heath was still alive. Cyril has put on worn wool pajamas, and is paging through his biographical dictionary again. He starts to slip into his bed.

I reach over and grasp his hand. "Cyril, come over into my bed with me. Please."

The poor man. I have surprised him. He seems almost terrified. Surely this possibility had occurred to him; he had grown silent as we prepared for bed, and averted his gaze as I changed into my gown, but now his dear, battered face is even ruddier than usual. I realize again that everything in this new/old life is a first for Cyril. I want to comfort him and caress him, to make things comfortable for my friend, but he is old and cannot be too abruptly surprised.

"Come, sweet man. I want you here beside me. It is all right to be close to each other. I would like it." He slips into bed beside me and pulls the covers up to his neck. I roll over and put my arm on him under the covers. He is trembling slightly. "It would be so fine to hold each other, Cyril. Let's do it. Let's be near each other. We are such good friends now; let us just warm each other with our bodies, too." I unbutton his pajama top and press toward him. He is breathing so hard and seems so bewildered it worries me. I don't want him to have a stroke or heart attack.

"Hush, hush, Cyril," I say as I slowly stroke his ribs with my fingertips. "This is good. Isn't it good? Relax and feel my touch. Now reach over and hug me; it is okay; we can embrace together and share our warmth. We've had a wonderful day. Let's relax and enjoy our closeness."

Lord knows what Cyril's thought about such things so alone in his long life. I don't want to think about it. But now he does take a light hold of me. "Why would anyone want to hold *me*?" he whispers and ducks his head against my chest.

"I want to hold you because you are my dearest, my only friend, Cyril. I have never known anyone like you. I want you to *know* that I trust myself to you. I like having your arms around me. It warms me and completes our friendship."

I'm not sure he really yet believes in himself. But yes, he holds me more tightly and kisses my forehead and cheek with an eagerness that, I believe, surprises him. I try to calm his breathing by placing my hand on his bare chest, then slipping it over his shoulder. I finish unbuttoning his pajama top and take his arms out of his sleeves. I hold him close, his trembling, battered, frozen and defrosted body.

"Now you must kiss my lips," I say, and he does this hesitantly but eagerly, and I am glad for his ardor, for his clumsy kiss, such late fulfillment for him.

I dare something more—perhaps I should not have—but I reach down through his pajama fly and grasp his limp penis. He exhales loudly and tosses his head, but I feel only a slight stirring in my hand.

I hasten to reassure him. "Oh, it is such a precious thing," I say as I gently stroke it. "It is dear—I like holding it." Again there is a slight rousing, but that is all. I wonder if I am being cruel—I don't want that. This is what we can do, and I believe it is very nice for him and for me to have this intimacy. We have so many other things together.

"Cyril," I say. "Now I want you to touch me." I unbutton my gown and guide his gnarled, shaking hand slowly to my breasts, then my vagina. "Just touch. Put your fingers on it and into it. Hush, my sweet man. It is all right. It is *all* right."

He does as I suggest, almost guiltily, but I whisper, "Thank you, Cyril. It makes me feel good to have you touch me. It is what I want, for us to be together like this, doing what we can do."

"You are so perfect," Cyril says. "So smooth." He has not, I am quite certain, ever said such things before in his life.

For still a while more we embrace, just stroking and holding, until finally Cyril's breathing eases and grows even. He is old and *nothing* can postpone his weariness any longer as he slips into unconsciousness. It has been a long, long adventuresome day. We have worn ourselves out being adrift in the world, and thus he slips into sleep, but does not take his arms away. I hold him in the darkness and we slumber together through the night.

How fine it is the next morning to wake in each other's arms, achy from the wine and wonderful excitement of the previous night. We are even a bit surprised, as lovers are sometimes, both of us, dehydrated, still tired, but happy to pay a little for our sins. We sip water, and I misquote from *Romeo and Juliet*, "Night's candles are burnt out, and jocund day/ Stands tipoe on the misty driftless hills."

After a brief interlude of caressing we finally stir ourselves and get dressed. I find the Madison classics station on the clock radio. As we wash and dress, we listen to some adventurous Corigliano; we take our many medicines, then go downstairs to the dining room.

A good breakfast of eggs Benedict (Cyril's first, he is wildly enthusiastic), huge glasses of orange juice, and pot of tea clears our heads. We chuckle with pleasure over memories of our wild capers of the night before, and agree that these newfound activities should continue, but be rationed and held for special occasions. We cannot play cozy in the home. That would be begging trouble. But we have impetus now to venture further.

In late morning we walk out and take a light lunch, pay our hotel bill, and stroll the streets of Madison awhile more before starting back. Things have gone well and we are quiet—two weary, happy old folks as we drive slowly back to Soldiers Grove. We become apprehensive as we near the home, hoping that no one has taken note of our overnight spree.

We decide to walk right back into the lobby as if nothing had happened and sneak our overnight bags in later. It is dinnertime when we arrive in the parking lot, and we know the staff is occupied; we walk in the front door, heading directly toward the dining area. An attendant is at the front desk, but she is speaking on the phone and barely notices us. We wave airily and hasten on.

In the dining room the meal is ham slices, corn niblets, and lumpy mashed potatoes. The singer is standing with her fingertips on the table, in the midst of a wavering but touchingly appropriate rendition of (yes, I risk credibility by claiming this as the solemn truth) "Last Night, When We Were Young." We smile and poke the food around on our plates. Our entertainer sounds more in touch than usual with her song. No one seems to have missed us and no one comes to accuse us; we have a sense of accomplishment, and are already scheming about even more far-flung adventures.

Liberty. Travel. Over the many years these things had become large abstractions for me. Freedom. But these words have taken substance again—with sweet, damaged Cyril as my partner.

When we pass by the front desk again on the way back from dinner the attendant suddenly hails Cyril, and we both stop in our tracks. Have we been overconfident? Are we uncovered? Cyril approaches the desk warily. He is told there is a phone message for him.

"For *me?*" Cyril asks. He has never received a phone message in his life.

"Here it is," the woman says. "It was taken down earlier by one of the afternoon volunteers. Maybe it's a prank," she says as she studies it.

The message reads: "Charlotte Brontë called. Please return her call." A number is scrawled below the message. We take the note back to Cyril's room; he dials and sets his phone volume high so I can hear what is being said.

"Oh, Cyril," Charlotte says when she hears his voice. "A man came into the bookstore today looking for you. He said he was an old friend and had heard you were in the hospital. He came to our store because he said he knows you are a bookish sort, and he thought it possible that we would know your whereabouts. He said he was concerned when he'd checked at the hospital and found you'd been discharged. The hospital doesn't give address information, so he's been scouting around for you. He was polite, but was such a large, rough-looking man, he intimidated Anne. I'm not sure she did the right thing—he was so imposing and made her feel so disengaged, she revealed that you are back in the home.

"He seemed . . . very determined. Anne is still upset by the incident. Emily is furious with Anne for telling him your whereabouts. Emily is always suspicious of everyone. She tried to move the man along without giving him any infor-mation, and he suddenly became very gruff with her and it frightened her that he might become physical. He called her 'sister' when he addressed her—and Emily hates that sort of reference. It boils her blood.

"Cyril, I'm afraid this man might show up sooner or later looking for you at the home, and we didn't want you to be surprised. I'm so sorry if we've done something wrong or caused difficulty for you," said Charlotte. "I hope he really is an old friend stopping through for a visit."

She waits for a moment for a response from Cyril. It does not come. "But I guess not," she says at last. Cyril thanks her for taking the message, hangs up, and turns to hold my hand.

CHAPTER 15

Cyril

It is Balaclava. The realization sends a shock down from my balls to my hobbled feet, then all the way back up my spine.

Lucifer himself! The monster. The one who left me to the eternal deep freeze. What in God's name does he want? What do I do now? Call the sheriff? Buy a gun?

Louise is a quick study. She recognizes the problem. "It's the man who put you out in the storm, isn't it?" she asks in alarm. "Cyril, you've got to call the police. That man is a dangerous fugitive!"

I try to be mister tough guy for Louise, but she can see that I am knocked flat. I start lurching around the room, forgetting to use my canes, stumble and almost go down. Louise grabs me and guides me back to my chair. She wants me to call the sheriff *now*. She looks up the number and I dial.

He answers his phone himself after one ring. "Yeah," he says, "sheriff." Perhaps he's out cruising and speaking to me on one of those little telephones that everyone carries now. Of course he remembers me from when he pulled me out of that pile of snow in the blizzard. The sheriff is the guy who saved my bacon when I was about to change into a block of ice. That whole episode has become one of the legends of these parts.

When I was in the hospital he came to ask me questions, but I was still loony, looking at the world through frosted glass, and I have no distinct memory of him.

When I tell him now that Balaclava might be back in town, he tells me he will come over immediately. We wait for him in the lobby of the rest home and he arrives in five minutes. "Mr. Solverson," the sheriff says, putting out his big paw for a shake.

I dimly recollect him from my frozen time, a substantial guy with a surprisingly high, but husky voice like Aldo Ray. He has a slight beer belly and his uniform fits him snuggly. His big-brimmed sheriff's hat is tilted forward almost to his eyebrows, and there's just the faintest ribbon of moustache over his mouth.

He looks me up and down. "I can see those docs rolled you over pretty good, Mr. Solverson. You doing okay?"

"Fair to middling," I say. "You know, I never did have a chance to thank you for what you did, but that blizzard got a piece of me. It took the docs a lot of time to finally get me put back together—it took all the king's horses and all the king's men. Now I've got this problem. That hood who snatched me and then put me out into the snow . . . I think he's back in town looking for me. I wish I knew why."

"That man is also wanted for armed robbery, stealing a truck, vehicular homicide, wounding a policeman, manslaughter, and a bunch of other things. I'd sure like to know if he's back in these parts."

Just the account of Balaclava's record chills me again, but I struggle on to tell the sheriff, "The Brontë sisters in Viroqua saw him. He was in their shop asking about me."

"Who are the Brontë sisters?"

"That's what we call those three women who own the bookstore."

The sheriff seems puzzled by this for a moment, but doesn't pursue. He asks, "When did they see him?"

"Yesterday. He really scared the hell out of them."

"Did he threaten them?"

"No. He was trying to act straight—but that guy can't help looking nasty, no matter which angle he turns. The nature of the beast."

~ 131 ~

"There's a *lot* of badass guys out there these days. Are you sure this is the same one who abducted you? What's he look like?"

"When he pushed me out into that whiteout he was wearing a fur hat over his whole head, but I saw he had gray eyes, and a mouth like a shark gill. He's big, big and big, has a muscle voice like Tami Mauriello."

"Who is Tami Mauriello?" the sheriff asks.

"Cyril!" Louise cautioned, sensing that my mechanism had been tripped.

But I had to tell the sheriff just a little about Mauriello. I can't help myself. I am Cyril, the tender of lives. "He was a heavyweight boxer, and he staggered Joe Louis with a punch one time, before Louis took him out."

"Not too many guys did that," the sheriff observes.

"He played in *On the Waterfront* with Marlon Brando, too. Not many guys did *that* either."

"Cyril, this is *serious* business!" Louise cautions.

The sheriff goes on with his questioning. "Why would this guy come back to Soldiers Grove looking for you? He must know there's a watch out for him."

"I don't know why he's here, but I am in no condition to be facing him down. Can you help me?"

"I'll put out a general alert, and I'll talk to those Brontë ladies and get a better description. Do you have any idea where he might be hiding?"

"I can't say," I reply, then, after a little reflection, "I suspect he's pretty good at keeping himself scarce until he's ready to pull one of his capers; he probably lives in vehicles, breaks into abandoned houses. He knows how to hang out in deep woods. I think I saw some camping gear behind the seat of his pickup, and we've got a lot of trees on these driftless hills. He knows how to disappear."

"Do you carry a cell phone?"

"No, sir."

"I don't have enough guys to assign you twenty-four-hour protection, but I'll get you a little alarm device that will signal us in case the guy comes around. Do you have a weapon?"

"No."

The sheriff sees my hesitation. "You better think about getting something. Even a knife, a blackjack or something."

"I couldn't bruise a peach, even with a blackjack in my hand."

"Too bad you don't know Tami Mauriello," the sheriff smiles.

But it isn't funny. This berserker is sniffing around Soldiers Grove again! He seems to be looking for me now. Louise looks scared. That makes me angry—I don't want Louise to be frightened. I'm so sorry she's been dragged into this thing.

"Watch yourselves," the sheriff says, and heads for the door.

Watch ourselves? Oh, *sure*! A couple of arthritic elders up against King Kong! If that goon walked in here now we couldn't do anything but slap at him and flash our snags. Together we might still be on our feet, but the two of us are no match for a mad dog. He'd as soon put me under as look at me. I've still got the chilblains to prove it. But what the hell does he want with me now?

CHAPTER 16

Louise

The sheriff has been checking in with us, and his deputy delivered the alarm device. They finally have a description of Balaclava produced in detail by the Brontë sisters who portrayed him as a sort of combination sloth bear and Gila monster.

The home administration, of course, talked to us at length about these recent happenings. They are almost as uneasy about the situation as we are. They do not want any trouble in the home. Elderly people are easily disturbed. Cyril and I don't wish to start a panic.

This is not a good time for us to try and slip out on one of our larks, so the Dodge remains discreetly parked in a far corner of the lot.

Finally Cyril and I take a scheduled home shuttle ride to Viroqua to visit the Brontë sisters in the bookstore. Cyril feels guilty for involving them in his trouble, and cannot apologize enough.

I noticed a story in the county newspaper about a holdup in one of the local bars. The robber was described as a large man who wore a ski mask covering his face. The prospect haunts us. Cyril has never imagined that he might end up a stalked man.

This quiet, sparsely populated area is not accustomed to this sort of thing. The sheriff visits us again and asks more questions. We are able to tell him very little. Again he suggests that Cyril obtain a weapon. This increases our uneasiness. Cyril has never touched a gun, and is very reluctant to do so now.

So I must *do* something. I slip out surreptitiously one afternoon while Cyril is napping and drive the Dodge to my farm. Heath kept weapons in the house from when he was a boy—a shotgun, a rifle, a small, pearl-handled revolver. Once he demonstrated to me how to aim the pistol, how to stand firmly with legs spread, hold the gun with two hands at arms' length, and sight down the barrel with one eye. He showed me how to load it and I fired it a few times for practice. I hated it—the intimidating bang, a tin can flying violently off the rock where Heath had placed it as a target.

But now I put the gun in my handbag with some bullets and bring it back with me to the home. When I show it to Cyril he becomes upset that I have done this. He will have nothing to do with the weapon.

Another week passes and there are no further robberies or demon signs. We allow ourselves a slight relaxation. Perhaps Balaclava has decided to abandon the territory. We do not have the nerve to try one of our daytime excursions in the truck, but Cyril is growing bored and restless. He suggests that we at least slip out and make our way over to Burkhum's Tap one evening for just one Leinenkugel.

CHAPTER 17

Cyril

I convince Louise that we've got to get out of the home for just a brief while to preserve our sanity and breathe free air. We've got the routine down. It's almost as simple as just walking out the door—but not quite. We still prop open an exit door with a piece of cardboard and make the break when the coast seems clear. This makes our exploits more exciting, and part of our pleasure is the stimulation of *escape*—believing that we've done something daring. We always chuckle gleefully as we hobble slowly across the road to the tavern.

I've had two Leinenkugels and Louise is nursing one. I feel so good I am about to signal for a third round when Louise firmly puts her hand over mine. "Cyril, we've got to keep our wits about us. These weeks have been challenging, and I don't believe it's over yet."

"How about splitting one with me?" I suggest. "I'll get a glass."

"Cyril, please keep a lid on. We can only hope that monster has moved on—but he came back here for some mysterious reason, and you certainly seem to be a big part of that reason."

This gives me a chill. I try to ignore the full meaning of what she is saying. "How about just a little something to get us back across the road?"

I like to hang on to that lovely early alcoholic glow. I once read an interview with a jazz musician—I can't remember who, maybe Lester Young—and he was talking about drinking. "I'd like to stay just slightly loaded all the time," he said. "Trouble is, I always get excited and start the spillover." That's where my parents were—permanently spilled over. "Okay, let's go home," I say to Louise.

I notice she has carried her little handbag with the pistol inside, and this gives me the willies. Louise has more sense of the present than I do. I tease her about it, "I notice you're packing your rod. So I'll feel safe. I can see the headlines now in the *National Enquirer*: BELLE STARR RETURNS FROM GRAVE TO SUBDUE ICEMAN'S ENEMY. Do you know who Belle Starr was?"

"Cyril, the Leinenkugel—it is making you silly. No brief lives now! Let's go. We've got to be careful."

"Belle Starr blew a lot of men away in her day. She was born in Missouri and fell in with Jesse James and Cole Younger, and was as tough as any of them."

"Cyril, I am *not* as tough as any of them. I'm an old French peasant woman who gets very worried. This is no time for brief lives. We've got to get back across that road without trouble."

"Okay, okay, you're right," I reach down to pick up our canes from under my chair. Our first small spat—and I want no more. I am *not* going to go where my parents went. We make our way through Burkhum's tables and head out.

It's a sweet night, a half moon still low enough so that we can see the high clear stars over the driftless hills. I'm sure there are crickets sawing on the shadows, but they don't resound in my one working ear. Okay, it probably wasn't a good idea to slip out to Burkhum's. I admit I'm a little nervous now, and I sense Louise's very real tension in the wide darkness. I regret I've caused her to be worried.

We hobble across the berm onto the road shoulder. No cars moving, so we tap-tap-tap across the pavement to the other side as quickly as we can. There is light coming from Burkhum's big sign and the two high, yellow utility lamps on poles over the rest home parking area. But darkness dominates, and as we step into the shadows of the trees and shrubs in the strip around the edge of the parking lot, something rustles in nearby greenery.

I can't quite make it out, but whatever it is, it is much bigger than a raccoon, much larger than a rabbit or coyote, about the size of a large deer, but not bigger than a bear. Whatever it is, it is definitely scrunching through the shrubs toward us. Louise makes a very small sound, but I am quiet. Both of us instinctively touch each other and continue our quick shuffle in the direction of the home away from the advancing specter.

By the time we trundle onto the pavement of the parking lot I notice that Louise—my God in heaven!—Louise has opened her little purse and has her pearl-handled pistol in her hand. How can things happen so fast? Here we were hobbling our way home under the stars, my tummy happily gurgling with Leinenkugel, and in a wink we are facing some heaping menace. Or at least Louise is confronting it. I am doing my very best to make her shuffle along; but Louise, brave, incredible Louise, is prepared to fight if necessary!

Whatever it is, this imposing shadow in the bushes, it hesitates before emerging, probably because it sees Louise's pistol—and just at that moment the whole area fills with light as a car swings down our lane of the parking lot, coming toward us with headlights on bright. The dark menace thrashes back through the shrubs away from us.

One, two, three—one, two, three—our canes tap as we hurry across the parking lot asphalt, making our plodding way, giving each other as much support as possible. No words pass as we dodder hurriedly toward the entrance. When we reach the home we are too weary and frightened to show any caution, and walk right in the front door together without hesitation. Thank God Louise has put her pistol away, and the woman at the desk is engrossed in a book and doesn't look up.

In our exhaustion we head for one of the lounge couches in a far corner and ease ourselves down to be close to each other. I take Louise's hand in mine and we put our heads together. We don't speak; we concentrate on slowing our breathing. It is such a comfort to be with each other.

I haven't the slightest conception of what young love is. I missed out on all that. I even missed out on middle-aged love. But I am learning about old love fast—and it is a very, very fine thing. Being close to Louise at this moment, her head on my shoulder, facing this crisis together—her proximity is the most meaningful thing that has ever happened to me in my life.

Cyril, I say to myself, you have *got* to do something to make yourself worthy of this woman!

CHAPTER 18

Louise

Whatever that monstrous thing was in the shrubbery, large or small, dark or light, it seemed to have very bad intentions. One could sense its malice as it moved toward us. It was not an animal, but a human being, a figure of fear and anger; otherwise why would it be lurking and approaching us in the dark? We were fortunate that the car came through the parking lot at that time and brought its light.

Cyril and I talk quietly in the lounge as we recover. He has the sheriff's emergency gadget in his pocket, and we discuss whether we should use it. But our situation is complicated by our culpability: we had gone out of the home against the rules—AWOL, I believe the military call it, away without leave—and we are wary of drawing the administration's attention to our mischief. We also hesitate to draw further awareness to our troubles with Balaclava. If they catch us breaking rules or if trouble happens, they could put us out. Where would we go then? Already the chief administrators are looking askance at us as if we are troublemakers.

In any event, what could the sheriff do if we called him? Go out and inspect the bushes with his flashlight? Two old fools out after dark against the rules, afraid of the bogeyman . . . Perhaps it *had* been an animal. Animals often wander through the landscape and woods of the driftless hills. An animal also would have run away from the light of the car.

When one feels under threat, darkness can delude you into enlarging on strange presences. That's how ghosts are born. That's how demonic creatures get into the world. But for now, neither Cyril nor I really believe that large shadow was an animal.

It is late. So we say goodnight with an embrace and go at last to our rooms to sleep the difficult sleep of elders. By mutual agreement, Cyril and I do not spend time complaining to each other—but both of us find the aging process to be vexing. My dreams are often disturbing. The link between the subconscious and unconscious is a slender strand—and sometimes in the middle of the night I cross back and forth like a courier between these states, then finally bear my bad dreams into consciousness to lie awake uncomfortably the rest of the night.

Now with our recent experiences I have even less confidence in the possibility of some hours of blessed sleep. I have pills which give some help, but their effect wears off easily. Once I awaken it becomes a struggle against the weariness that is omnipresent. If I am able to drop back to sleep, my dreams are sometimes nightmares from which I feel I might never escape.

For instance, here is the very worst of my bad reoccurring dreams: A doctor has given me a battery of medical tests and is reviewing results with me. I can see him growing uneasy as he talks. At last he looks at me desolately and gives me the word. He tells me I am incurably ill, that nothing else can be done—it is a matter of months. When I recover from the shock of his announcement and have had time to think, I tell the doctor I am resolved to death, but I do not wish to delay it. If it is inevitable—then I wish to have it now. Can it happen without all the dreary waiting?

"That is your choice then," the doctor says in the dream. He scribbles a prescription, rips it from his pad and hands it to me. I put it in my small purse where I now keep the pistol.

I wait a few days and my condition worsens. Finally I put on my coat and struggle to the pharmacy to have the prescription filled, coming home with a bottle of oddly opaque liquid. The label reads:

DEATH.

Take two tablespoons at night on an empty stomach. There is no prescription number for renewals. There is a small yellow sticker pasted to the bottle. It reads, *Warning: This medicine will cause visual dimming and ultimate closure.*

I have made my decision. Without further hesitation, I take up a tablespoon, fill it to the brim with this liquid and swallow, then pour a second and take it down fast. *DEATH* has no taste, it goes smoothly down my throat, immediately entering my head and heart. I feel chill waves begin to move across my intestines, my sight dims, my heart staggers, my fingers have no feeling—but I do not die. There is no ultimate darkness. Things just become grayer and more distant.

I grow impatient and frightened that I will end up only impaired. Spilling and shaking, I struggle to take two more tablespoons of *DEATH*, attempting to hasten its process, feeling it edge down my capillaries, creep into my heart and brain. Now things are shutting down all over my body.

Suddenly I grow frightened, feel a loneliness beyond comprehension. I will miss life! Yes. Yes. I will miss Cyril. I wish I had not been so impulsive. I struggle desperately against the dream, clawing my way out of it, and wake up just before I die, steeped in sweat, gasping and clutching the sheets.

I find my dream so frightening and feel so shaken by it that later, in a rare disclosure, I tell Cyril of the experience.

He takes hold of me and hugs me warmly to calm my trembling. Then he excuses himself for a moment and disappears into the vending area, returning with a small carton of chocolate milk, placing it in my hand. He is smiling. He knows I love chocolate milk. It is my brown balm, my panacea. He even reaches to spread the cardboard spout open for me.

The presence of Cyril is a miracle. How could I have predicted that such a person might come into my life exactly at this late, critical point, someone who would bring me chocolate milk when I need it most? Without Cyril, I would have perished of ennui. With Cyril, I have marvelous adventures, someone to love and hold and trust again, someone with whom I can face down troubles and fears.

Chapter 19

Cyril

What does Balaclava want with me now? Why is he here again? What will he do if he catches me this time—douse me with kerosene and set me on fire?

That fiend still has his ferocious gun, and he's been robbing people with it. We are unarmed—except for Louise and her pearl-handled pistol. How can I allow this to happen— Louise to be my protector? Cyril, I say to myself, what kind of a wimp are you? For God's sake—*do* something to fight this dragon!

I have always distrusted guns. I used to go nuts when hunting season started in the driftless hills—all the blasting and boom-booming, the pickups full of bloodied corpses of dead deer.

I remember the summer when I was hiding from my drunken parents and reading the book of Shakespeare plays. There is a character in one of the Henry plays named Hotspur who thinks he is tough, and is always acting angry and poor-mouthing guys who choose not to arm themselves, calling them "popinjays and cowards."

Hotspur is like Danderman—a macho idiot. The percentages are literally dead wrong with guns. If you have a gun, there is always a more-than-even chance that you will shoot it sometime. When you shoot it, there's always a chance that a bullet is going to hit someone or something, causing terrible damage. That's the way I feel about it. Even my father, with his drunken temper, at least had the good sense to never have a gun in our house. I thank the Lord there was no family pistol for me to inherit when my parents died; I would have felt a responsibility to keep it in my sock drawer with some bullets—an American heirloom. Before I met Louise, feeling so hopelessly lousy and wracked with my ruined body, there were days when I would have considered rising from my bed and using a gun, if I'd had one.

But now, with Balaclava on the prowl again, apparently looking for me, I've got to do something, even if it's just to show Louise that I have *some* substance. I am thinking about Louise when I head in to the lunchroom and look for her at our usual table.

Danderman is sitting beside her, trying to bend her ear. She has her head down over her plate of fish sticks and soggy french fries, and is pushing diced carrots and peas around with her fork. I don't know whether it's anger or anxiety I feel when I see Danderman sitting with her. Louise smiles at me, "Hello, Cyril."

Danderman gives me his patronizing, ex-quarterback look, "Hey, chief," he says, "I hear you got a bogeyman after you." I'm surprised by this and turn to Louise. She shakes her head, meaning she's not the one who told him—so the rumor mill in the home is grinding. Danderman *gets* to me. He is such an asshole I want to give him a whack up the side of his goddamned head with my cane. It would be good practice for facing Balaclava. But Louise is sitting there, urgently smiling.

Danderman feigns concern for me. "Who's this guy who's after you?" he asks. "If it's a bill collector, maybe I could give you some help? Do you have a gun?"

The sneering gall of the guy! Hotspur! His whole life has been devoted to showing people up. I'm so angry I can barely speak, and end up saying something that sounds weak and simple-minded: "I think I can handle it myself."

Now I'm wondering about the talk that's been going around the home. The administrators have said they were going to try and keep a lid on this situation so that other residents wouldn't become frightened, but there's obviously been a leak, and I'm sure Danderman has done his part to promote the rumors.

He's looking at me with his condescending smile, bordering on a sneer. "Maybe we could work up a posse," he says. "We could call ourselves the Geezer Gang, or something." He laughs aloud at his own stupid wit. "We'll smoke this guy out and save your butt. Do you want me to see what I can do about organizing this? We could be the Crutch Crushers! The Mature Mob!" He laughs again and looks at Louise, hoping for a giggle from her, but Louise is looking at him as if he were a leprous skunk.

"This is not funny!" she says sharply. "Have you ever been stalked? You'd probably wet your security diaper."

Whoaa—my Louise! *Right* in the teeth! Danderman sits up straight in his chair like he's been coldcocked. He's not lipping off anymore; he's been nailed by a pretty woman. He's not used to having ladies give him the bird. He doesn't know whether to shit or go blind. Louise solves his dilemma for him. She rises from her chair, takes up her cane and tap-taps away, leaving her dinner uneaten.

I get up from the table, too. Danderman looks stunned and overheated. I think about fanning him with my paper napkin, but instead I take my plate and dump the fish sticks and french fries into his. "Enjoy," I say, and give him the crooked prong of my right middle finger, curl my frozen lip, and limp away out of the room.

There's a hunting and sporting goods store in Viroqua, and I ask Louise to drive me there in the Dodge. I pull out one of the socks full of cash from under my mattress and take out a small wad. As always, we slip out of the home like fugitives, but I'm not sure our stealth is necessary anymore. The home staff is looking the other way—I think it is pretty well agreed amongst them now that they will ignore us until we really screw up. I suspect they might even know we are keeping a vehicle in the parking lot.

Before we go to the gun shop we stop by the bookstore to see how the Brontë sisters are doing. They are glad to see us and express concern about our situation. The presence of Balaclava has everyone on edge.

"It's like having a Frankenstein monster loose in the community," Charlotte says. "Where will he turn up next? I wish there were some angry villagers around to light torches and help us pursue him."

I don't tell the Brontë sisters about our encounter with the beast in the bushes; but, of course—being who I am—I pick up on the Frankenstein tag. "Did you know that when they were shooting the first Frankenstein movie Boris Karloff got a skin condition from wearing all that monster makeup for hours on end? He had back problems, too, and had a hell of a time hauling that heavy costume around with him. It nearly killed him. That's kind of interesting when you think about it—the noble savage always trying to destroy his maker, even if it's only with makeup in a Hollywood movie."

I'm not sure the story about Karloff is quite true, but I thought it was interesting and sounded "literary" in the bookstore, and might help divert the Brontë sisters from being frightened.

Louise is browsing in the history section, but she turns around and gives me an incredulous look. But hell . . . for all I know it could be true! The Brontës like this sort of story anyway.

But I cut myself off before I can tell them about Karloff being born in East Dulwich, England, dropping out of Cambridge, and bumming around until he stumbled onto acting.

The old dropout even recorded some Shakespeare in his day. I spare everybody these details.

I don't want to speak too much about my experience in the gun shop, but I admit, it boggled my boggler to see all those weapons lined up on the walls, every kind of long gun, short gun, big gun, small gun, and handgun you can imagine. Colts, automatics, all varieties of scoped rifles, AK-47s and other assault weapons, muzzle-loaders, flintlocks, Lugers, shotguns of all varieties, and other violent-looking things right out in the open, lined up in rows on the wall for the public to see and buy. It seemed to me the store could arm a couple battalions and Viroqua could fight its own war. Maybe they could take on Westby or Soldiers Grove in pitched battle! The store stocks bows and arrows and even a few spears. Probably there are hand grenades under the counter.

When I see all this ordnance, all I want to do is get out of the place. But I came vowing to purchase a weapon to protect Louise and myself. Finally I let them sell me a pistol that I can manipulate with my arthritic right hand, a box of ammunition, and a shoulder strap so, if I choose to, I can wear the gun hidden under my jacket or shirt. I peel the money from my wad of cash. When the owner sees all the dough I am holding, he tries to also sell me one of his rifles.

No, no, no!

I have to fill out some registration papers for the gun, and my hand is shaking. I don't have a driver's license, so I use my health card, which has an identification picture on it. I find a certain irony in this.

So now I am an armed man. Those people would have sold me any weapons I wanted. I could have become an archfiend with an Uzi. A mad sharpshooter in a bell tower with a scoped rifle. Now I could take little bullets out of a box, put them into my gun (which the proprietors have carefully shown me how to load), walk out on the street and kill as many people as I want. Blow them clean away. Six at least before I'd have to reload. I wouldn't even have to think about the lives I was snuffing out. Just boom, boom, boom! It's over for them. When you're dead, you're down and *dead*. You could be a politician, a violinist, a jeweler, a clerk, a bum, a lawyer, a liberal, a conservative, a poet, a gang leader, the best singer in the world. Boom! You're dead, and I did it. You're *dark*.

Who you lookin' at, boy? Don't you recognize Big Cyril? Know who you're talking to, buddy! Boom!

Now that I have this thing, what am I going to do with it? Carry it around under my shirt in the shoulder holster like a hit man? It makes no sense to just leave it in my room if we are trying to protect ourselves. Louise is carrying her gat in her purse, too.

Louise and Cyril. Bonnie and Clyde.

Go ahead. Make my day. Boom! So long sucker.

My God! What will become of us all? Our species must have crawled out of the ocean onto the beach eons ago with guns already in our claws.

Arthur Koestler! Now *there* was a guy. Born in Hungary, he went through political and social hell; he escaped, adopted the English language, and wrote hard stuff about whether the human race was going to make it through. He'd seen it all. Someone asked him once, after reading one of his doom books—what might preserve our species? He suggested that we consider permanently tranquilizing the whole human race.

CHAPTER 20

Louise

Buying the gun has its curious effect on Cyril. It's not that he grows surly, but he seems disappointed in himself, as if he has at last given in to the waltz with death, the violence in the world which has always horrified him, and at last tossed his lot in with the thugs.

It had been such an easy thing for him to do, walk into that shop and become an armed person. Before this, Cyril walked innocently in this world, sharing his brief lives with people, drinking his Leinenkugel, being his affable, reclusive self. Now that he has discovered how easy it is to become owner of a lethal weapon, he looks at other people differently, feeling certain that almost everyone is packing "protection" under their coats.

Dear, guileless Cyril, permanently maimed by his wretched childhood, he has made his life so vicarious. He has never been violent, but he has been on occasion fascinated by the aggression he finds in some of the brief lives he holds in his mind.

I have no idea whether Cyril has ever thought much about sex, or considered it as a possibility for himself.

But of course he has—of *course* he has. It always seems to excite him when he refers to it in one of his brief lives—but his brief lives are surrogate-like films or literary images. How can I help him?

I admit that much of my own life also has been displaced and lived remotely as a sort of solitary ersatz artist. I developed my own system of "brief lives," living a quasi-artistic life in the remoteness of the driftless hills, entering the lives of the writers, musicians and artists whose work I love to witness. No one was ever aware of my artistic interests and activities—except for Heath, who was also in his way guileless, who stayed by me as much as he was able, cared for my well-being, always made strong efforts to understand what I was thinking and doing.

Now I want to show Cyril some of the true artifacts and products of the brief artistic lives that *I* have known and studied. I plan carefully for several weeks—then one day invite him for an afternoon tea in my room. "Let's do something different," I say.

Cyril knows this will be a special event, but doesn't know quite what to expect. He appears at my door a little wary and nervous, with his sparse hair combed and boots shined, a new white shirt buttoned to his throat, and even a bright blue bow tie clipped crookedly to his collar. I am charmed. He has never been to a tea.

I purchased scones and good butter at the co-op grocery in Viroqua, and also prepared some cucumber sandwiches, cutting off the crusts. The tea is Earl Grey, with milk warmed in the pitcher, and there are cubes of sugar with little spoons. I have selected some poetry, art books and music cassettes that I think might interest Cyril. Things that are very dear to me, but unfamiliar to him. He is apprehensive.

Always full of lives, when he sees my tea tray he is somehow prompted to start telling me his brief life of Henry James, apparently because he knew James enjoyed small, civilized events like teas.

"Henry James came from a big family of very smart people," Cyril starts. "He always felt a little inferior. After he finished law school at Harvard he fooled around for a while, then escaped from his imposing family and moved to Europe in 1875 and really bore down on writing fiction . . ."

"No, no, no, Cyril!" I protest gently. "Not today. No brief lives. You must be quiet and focus on what I want to show you. This is *my* afternoon."

He looks chastened, so I hasten to reassure him, patting him on his crabbed hand—but I know he will be quiet now. I pour two cups of Earl Grey from the pot and pass him the milk and sugar. He puts in three cubes and splashes milk into his cup. His hand is shaking.

"Dear Cyril, please relax, this is *not* a test, and I'm not trying to intimidate you. We are friends forever, no matter what. I just want to try and share some of the things I love because I think you might enjoy them."

I take up my well-thumbed copy of the collected poems of A. E. Housman, a poet lyrical and direct, who often wrote about the countryside. I don't want to start with writing that is too complicated, and I don't want Cyril to feel challenged. I hope that he will begin to hear things in the lyrics, sounds of the words and lines.

Cyril sees the writing on the book cover. "Ah yes," he says. "Alfred Edward Housman was born in Fockbury, Worcestershire, in 1859 and his stuff got really popular during the First World War . . ."

"Cyril!" I say emphatically, and silence him. "Please, please relax. Just listen to this. It is one of his *poems*, let the words and sounds come to you":

> *Loveliest of trees, the cherry now*
> *Is hung with bloom along the bough,*
> *And stands about the woodland ride*
> *Wearing white for Eastertide.*
>
> *Now, of my threescore years and ten,*
> *Twenty will not come again,*

And take from seventy springs a score,
It only leaves me fifty more.

And since to look at things in bloom
Fifty springs are little room,
About the woodlands I will go
To see the cherry hung with snow.

As I read it aloud, I am concerned that Cyril might not absorb some of the very British images in the poem—but he is quiet only for a few moments. He is thinking, then he asks, "Would you read that again?"

Bless his beautiful heart! I read the poem again. Cyril moves his right hand slightly with the rhythm as I read. When I am finished, he says, "That's almost like singing a small song—your voice is beautiful when you read it. It's quiet and watchful. Housman is not trying to give us a big story, but he shows a lot by just saying some of those words—bough, trees, cherry, bloom, spring, woodlands, and the nice surprise at the end with snow. There's sadness in the poem about being young and getting old. It's like he's taking me by the hand and leading me through that English springtime. And you lead me, too, Lady Louise, under the boughs and cherry trees, with the way you read, I got the music with the words. That's all pretty special."

Oh, Cyril! Indispensable, hideously adorable Cyril! If I could live fifty springs more just to be with you, I would do it.

"Would you like more tea?" I ask him. "Try the scones. They are good." I pour him another cup and he butters a scone and puts it on his plate.

He looks at my little stack of books. "Would you read some more, please?" he asks. I would hug him, but his tea would spill. Instead, I read a Robert Frost poem, a John Clare, Wallace Stevens, Pablo Neruda, I read translations into English of Charles Baudelaire and Stéphane Mallarmé. Cyril gives me only very abbreviated biographies of each of these poets, then listens carefully as I read. I even include an Arthur Rimbaud poem, reading "Delirium" to Cyril in French, then translating it into English for him:

> Ce fut d'abord une etude. J'écrivais des silences
> des nuits, je notais l'inexprimable. Je fixais
> des vertiges.
> "At first it was experimenting. I wrote of silences in
> the night, I recorded the inexpressible. I fixed
> their dizzy flight . . ."

I read the whole poem to him.

"So *that's* Rimbaud?" Cyril says in wonder when I finish. "Listen to that guy! He's hustling danger in that poem, and fixing himself for a big fall. He must have been on opium all the time, and God knows what else. You can hurt yourself that way, you know, and I guess he did. But it was like he was *trying* to hurt himself. I know he was nineteen when he gave up poetry and took off for Abyssinia and tried to be a gunrunner. He got a dose there and didn't live much past his midthirties."

Precious, amazing Cyril, he knows the brief life of Arthur Rimbaud—but he has never read one of the poems. What a rare afternoon! The two of us come together like a locking jigsaw puzzle. Here we are, two American ancients reading the hallucinatory poetry of a precocious, perilous eighteen-year-old French boy written 150 years ago. And we are a team. Where else would such mysteries like this be happening in this large world, except in Soldiers Grove?

I read Cyril another section from *Une Saison en Enfer*, and he comments when I am finished, "That boy was giving us something when he stuck his head in the fire like that, almost as if he were feeding himself to terrible dreams. He seemed to want to explore all the possibilities and then go down with his ship and tell us about it before he grew old."

To conclude the poetry, I read something briefer and gentler—a translation of Tu Fu:

> *March is gone, and April here.*
> *How many more chances to welcome spring?*
> *Do not think of things beyond death;*
> *Just drain these last allotted cups of life.*

"It's almost like he is talking directly to the two of us," Cyril comments. "He is saying good-bye with only a few words, before he says hello again from 1,300 years ago."

I want to play some music for Cyril. The afternoon is short and I have to be selective, so start with small pieces or short movements from Mozart, Debussy, Mendelssohn. He listens hungrily, happily, and always, without hesitation, makes some comments.

This is Cyril on Debussy's fifth Étude: "He pops right into that, doesn't he? Gives a theme and works it over hard a few times, then runs his tune like a horse. People were still running around on horses in those days, and a lot of that galloping sound gets into his music. I heard it in the Mendelssohn you played, too. That pianist is quick! A statement with a theme; he gets it all in there. Debussy's very French, isn't he? He starts fast, then slows to a trot before he surprises us by galloping on some more. He's got to be firm in the saddle. He gets a lot done in that little bit of time, doesn't he? What is an étude?"

Cyril, so swift sitting there—looking like a bear burned in a forest fire—takes my breath away. What could he have been if he'd had half a chance? It doesn't matter. He is the keeper of the lives—and that is worth more than three advanced degrees or a billion dollars.

"An étude is a brief exercise, I guess you would call it," I tell him. "Like a hop, skip, and jump in a track meet. It's meant to give the pianist a chance to show off."

It's getting late in the afternoon. I had wanted to show Cyril some painting reproductions and had taken out a stack of big art books. But there was really only time to show him one artist, so I select the relatively unknown Gustave Caillebotte, whose work has always intrigued me. An odd choice amongst the French galaxy of painters—but then Cyril and I are both odd choices, too. We page together through the book, admiring the painter's skill and energy. Cyril particularly likes Caillebotte's painting of workmen scraping a floor in some building, their weariness evident in late afternoon.

There is only half-light in my room now. I switch on several lamps. I had wanted to play some of the jazz I love for Cyril, too, and hear his comments—perhaps Lester Young or Thelonious Monk, but it has grown too late, and we are tired. We've learned a great deal about each other in these hours. I will host many more teas for the two of us, I promise him. Cyril is finishing a second scone.

"Perhaps we better stop eating," I say. "We're going to be too full for our dinners."

"I hope so," Cyril says.

Chapter 21

Cyril

We buzz into the dining room just in time for the end of dinner service. Crumbled hamburger cooked with Wisconsin cheddar and topped with a tomato sauce, corn from a can, and two boiled potatoes—not exactly tournedos Rossini—but I give it a go. Louise is a little slower getting to it, poking her fork around, but eventually she digs in, too. The singer is working on her rendition of "Falling In Love With Love." Fortunately, she got it started right and is not off-key, so she doesn't sound half bad tonight. Sometimes she can reach back into herself and hit some of those notes pretty good.

We're both sleepy after our afternoon of culture and no naps—but we've had a time, a wonderful time, and will sleep well tonight. I notice Danderman a few tables over, trying to put some moves on an attractive, recently admitted widow. She doesn't look very interested. In fact, she looks as if she's not hearing most of what he says. Danderman yammers on, trying to look cool, a man of dogged habits.

Louise and I have talked a lot this afternoon, so we don't have much to say to each other at dinner. It's often like this when the day is done—a weariness that takes full possession of us. I see the same thing in the protracted movements of the other home guests sitting around us—a sort of heavy cloud that comes into the institution and bears down on us when light falls; we are a roomful of old folks in various stages of decay; the faint glimmering in our eyes that might have been present in the morning is obscured almost completely now. It is a time of day when, if you are going to get a disease, or feel the beginning of some kind of attack, or get a fever—it happens now. Days are generally okay, but when night inches in, the trolls seem to slip out from under the bridges around Soldiers Grove and creep into town to do mysterious things, and mostly they head for this old folks' home.

After the dining hall we all return to our rooms. A little television, medicines, and wash-ups, then there is only one thing to do—go to bed and begin the cramped tussle between consciousness and bizarre subconscious dreams, interrupted by trips to the john. You piece together the best sleep you can—just suck it up and go on. Some folks are better at this than others. Louise and I do okay, but we've had a lot of things on our minds these past days and weeks.

The dessert that evening in the dining hall is canned fruit salad. Louise picks out only the maraschino cherries, but I eat it all. We touch shoulders as we shamble through the corridors to our rooms; we're still glowing a bit from our very special day. I take her to her door, make sure no one is looking, give her a big hug and a small kiss, thank her for the tea, take in her astonishing smile one more time, and then, happy as an ant milking aphids, head off for my own digs.

As usual I haven't locked my room; I close the door behind me and hustle straight into the bathroom just inside to take an urgent pee and wash my hands, and when I come out to switch on the lamp over the couch I sense that somebody is in the room, sitting in the chair in the far shadowed corner.

I don't make any sound, but I take a step back, drop my canes, and almost fall over. A large, vile-looking shape in the corner shadows—I begin to see it more clearly as my eyes adjust to the light. An ogre with dirty hair all over his face and neck. It looks as if someone has slashed a mouth into his face with a flick knife.

"Well, well, well, geezer," Balaclava rumbles. "I see you are still peeing all the time. But you're changed since the last time I saw you. Did somebody run over you with a hay rake?"

I take another teetering backward step. "How did you get in here?"

"I walked right in like the local undertaker does every day. That desk attendant always has her nose in a book, and you left your door unlocked. I could have driven a Hummer in here and they wouldn't have known."

"Get out of here! I'll pull the emergency cord."

"It's already cut, gramps. Don't start talking tough. I think you better sit down. We've got some serious things to discuss."

But I choose to continue standing on my uneasy pegs. "What do you want with me?" My new little gun is strapped under my shirt, but I'd never be able to get it out in time. He'd be all over me if I started fumbling for it.

"Pops, you caused me a whole peck of trouble. Ever since I left you out in that blizzard the fuzz have been hot on my ass. It's given me fits trying to stay clear of them. But you— you make it through that storm and hang on long enough for the cops to find you.

"Then when everyone finds out you are going to pull through and defrost, they make you into a national hero! I thought they were going to give you the fucking Medal of Honor before they were through! All that ink they were giving you and they went on and on about how you were so goddamned courageous. Courageous, my *ass*! You were sucking your thumb. Big brave shit-ass! You were shaking and peeing your pants in my truck.

"Then the pictures of you in the paper, smiling like you'd just eaten a dozen chili dogs. They give you that goddamned award for *bravery*—50,000 smackers and a tuxedo dinner in New York! Bravery! Your pants were wet, old man! You were begging for mercy—and I *gave* you mercy. I let you go and made you famous. Do *I* get a 50,000-clam award for giving you mercy? Naw! They are chasing me down like a dog. You owe me big time, geezer man. Big time! Where's that money they gave you?"

"I can't remember."

Balaclava is up out of his chair and rolling toward me like a jagged boulder from the shadows. *Cyril*, I say to myself—as I did when I was about to be put out into that blizzard—*Cyril, this is it. All the lives in this world aren't going to save you now.*

Balaclava claps onto my shoulders and starts shaking me. My head is bobbing like an apple in high wind and I almost black out. "Wait, wait," I manage to gargle. "Don't kill me. That won't help. Let me think."

He lets go of me and sits down on the edge of my bed, breathing hard. The money is right under his ass, in two socks tucked under the mattress. I know this . . . but he doesn't. I fall onto the rug, and he's looking down at me. I try to make it look like I'm completely vulnerable—but I'm thinking fast. "I put it in the bank in Viroqua," I manage to whimper. He picks me up again like a broken twig, backhands me across my face, and tosses me onto the couch.

"Then you better figure how you can get it the fuck out of there so you can give it to me and save your ancient carcass. I want *all* of it!"

"I spent some of it."

"Don't give me that shit!" I wince because I think he is going to grab me again and start shaking. "What were you spending it on? Viagra? I seen you running around with that old cutie. I want all that goddamned money, geezer. *All!* Get it?"

I am thinking—how can anything so big and evil stay hidden? But Balaclava seems to manage. Apparently he can tuck himself away like a mortal sin in the darkest places, and then come out of the wallow to strike again.

I thought again about the small gun against my ribs. But I'm so slow and fumble fingered, I would die surely if I tried to reach into my shirt and pull it out. Everything would go.

"I can't get the money now," I say. "It's in the bank in Viroqua, and it's closed until tomorrow morning."

Balaclava looks like he's going to pitch another fit, so I lower my head. But he manages to calm down. "Okay, Pops. Then I'll spend the night with you, smelling your stale piss. And that is not going to put me in a better mood. Hanging around in the boonies watching old shitheads fall down all the time is not my favorite thing to do. So we are going to move this thing along; in the morning you *will* get your rickety ass over to that bank and withdraw the dough, and give it to me."

"I don't have a car. How am I going to get to Viroqua?"

"Get the goddamned limousine to take you! Get your little honey to drive you over. I been watching this place for a while. Don't screw around with me, gramps! I know how it all works and how you work. No tricks! You wouldn't want your sweetie to get all messed up, would you? I could make her look like mangled red cabbage."

He's really got my attention now. He looks at me carefully. "I seen how much you like her," he says slowly. Lights are going off in my head, I feel my heat going up. I almost go for my gun right then. My blood is pumping and my old claws are twitching. But if I die, it will only be hell to pay for Louise. I watch Balaclava thinking and it scares me.

I remember then the sheriff's little warning mechanism. What the hell have I done with it? I think I put it in the drawer of my bedside table, but I can't be sure. How can I get to it now? I can't be rooting around in drawers. I should have carried the thing with me. What a hopeless old idiot!

I can almost hear the gears meshing inside Balaclava's huge, oily head. The cogwheels finally click into place. My back hurts and my legs are cramping now. I am so angry and afraid, *knowing* what he's going to say next. I feel so helpless.

Balaclava says very slowly: "In fact, I think you better go get your little cookie jar right now and bring her back to this room. She can spend the night with us, too. That will make the cheese more binding. Isn't that what they do in Wisconsin? It should be real cozy, the three of us together for the night."

Why don't I just reach under the mattress and give him the money right now? I don't know. My God, I *don't* know! Because he would just knock me off anyway before he takes off with it—and kill Louise as a witness on his way out. Because it's the most money I have *ever* had in my life. But mostly because I have decided to use it to surprise Louise and treat her with a trip to France. That's the biggest reason of all. They gave the money to me because I was brave. If I'm so goddamned brave, then I don't want this perverted ball of hairy dung to have a dime of it!

He shows me his weapon then, slides it out of a long pocket in his boot, under his fat pant leg.

My God, that gun! Everything changes in the room when that gun comes out. I've never seen anything like it before—a long pitiless thing that looks like the devil's penis, with an attachment on the end of the barrel that seems to be a silencer. As he slips in a long clip of bullets, the darkness in the room consumes even more light. Everything is dimmer and seems more hopeless.

He says, "If you aren't back here in five minutes *exactly*, I'm coming after you. I mean it, geezer; and while I'm coming I'll kick down some doors and start taking out a whole lot of other old lizards. Remember, I've got *nothing* to lose. Then I'm going to blow the two of you away, too. But slow, one at a time, her first, with shots in the legs and guts before she really gets it in that pretty face. So you can watch. Does that make you know I'm serious, geezer? Think of your baby's face caving in when I blow it off with my cannon. You *know* I mean it!"

I grind my stubs of teeth. My ancient eyeballs boil in their sockets. I am thinking murder. I am thinking total violence. My gray fists clench painfully. I want to grind this creature up like a hog. But if I went for my pop gun now I wouldn't get past the top buttons of my shirt. I'd be spattered on the wall like an action painting, and Louise would be next. I have never felt such helplessness. He knows where she is. There are no doors for brutes like Balaclava.

He is nudging me hard with his huge weapon. "Get your ass rolling, old man. I'm looking at your clock. Get her back here in five minutes or everything goes!" Balaclava goes to the door, opens it and checks the hall, then shoves me out on my canes. I almost fall down.

I move as fast as I can, scrabbling along the corridor. I rap urgently below Louise's room number. I can hear her stirring slowly, getting out of bed. She speaks wearily through her door, "Who is it?"

"It's Cyril. Louise, please, quick. There's trouble." She opens, and I reach to take her arm. "Don't ask questions now. I'm so sorry. So sorry. Just come with me." She slips into her robe, takes her cane from behind the door and we slide and shuffle down the hall together as fast as we can. I feel her rising tension when she looks at me. She quickly senses what's going on.

My room door is slightly ajar; we push it open and falter in. Balaclava is behind it, and shuts it firmly. Now both of us are in his wicked hands. I ask myself again, should I just give him the money? But I know, even if I handed it over, he would shoot us as witnesses anyway, and God knows what else he would do.

Chapter 22

Louise

The beast signals us with his gun to move to the dim center of the room and points to the couch. We sit down.

So this is Balaclava. He is everything Cyril has described to me—hirsute and hideous, with a look that would freeze a ticking clock. How did this creature come into our lives? The door is shut, the room is small, and we are ensnared by this reeking monster.

"Hello, sister," he says, as offensively as possible, "I thought you'd like to join this little discussion. We're talking about money."

Some sort of ransom that he's demanding from Cyril? I look at Cyril and see how wary and pensive he is. He has a bleeding cut over his left eyebrow, a big bruise on his cheek. I reach to comfort him.

"No touching!" the sloth bear snarls. He points to Cyril. "The iceman here, he understands this now; he is going to get the money from the bank for me tomorrow morning. A whole lot of money. So we are all going to spend the night here together before we make the trip to Viroqua to get it. Ain't that cozy? And we are going to keep our goddamned mouths shut, and we are going to behave ourselves, aren't we, sister? Because any funny stuff that you try means that I start pulling this trigger, and once the two of you are all chewed up, I'm gonna walk down the hall and knock off as many old fogies as I can find on my way out.

"So we're going to keep our pretty mouth shut, aren't we, precious? And we are not going to try any tricks or make any signals. Right?" He turns to Cyril, "What time does that Viroqua bank open in the morning, pee-pants?"

"Nine o'clock," Cyril tells him. "But there's something else you should know."

"What the fuck is that?"

"The money is not deposited in a bank account. I cashed the check when I got the award, took the money in cash, and rented a safe-deposit box for it."

"What kind of hair-brained bullshit are you trying to give me now? Why would you do that?"

"I just don't like writing checks. I like cash," Cyril says.

The brute thinks about this and is greatly agitated. I fear he's going to assault Cyril again. I don't know what this money is that they are discussing or whether it exists. Cyril might be taking a big chance, just trying to get the beast out of here. Balaclava is out of his chair and standing in front of Cyril now, waving his ultimate weapon. "Are you playing games with me, gramps?"

"There's something else I might as well tell you now." Cyril has lowered his head, as if expecting another blow. "I can't remember where I put the bank-box key."

The monster roars and rams the tip of his gun hard against Cyril's cheek. Cyril slips over against me, but makes no noise. I can see he's bleeding from another cut and blood is coming from his mouth. I take the Kleenex from my robe pocket and dab at his wound. "You pig! If you keep hitting him, the people at the bank will wonder why he's all beaten up when he comes in!" I raise my voice. "He's doing his best!"

Beast thinks about giving me a whack, too, but some-how calms himself. He points at Cyril's drooping head. "He's gonna look like he's just been to the junior prom compared to the way he'll look like if he doesn't find that key! Where is it, frosty? Goddamn it! Start thinking fast."

"How is he going to think if you keep smashing him?" I snap, and continue to pat Cyril's wound.

"Grandma," Balaclava says slowly, "you need to understand this *very* clearly. This is not patty-cake going on here. Your lover boy is in a very bad situation. It would be best if you just keep your trap shut tight or you are also going to end up as a very wilted old flower."

He pulls a chair up to where Cyril is sprawled on the couch and pokes his gun barrel under Cyril's chin to push his head up. "Grandpa," he says, "it is time for you to do some serious remembering. You better think where that key is soon or I will really bring the curtains down. You aren't fucking with me, are you, geezer?" He pushes Cyril in the chest with his gun, but doesn't strike him again.

Cyril is slow in response. "I'm an old man. No matter what you do to me—I will forget things." Beast is tapping the tip of his huge weapon in his palm and breathing hard. Finally Cyril says shakily. "You've got to let me look around this room. There are some places where I might have put it."

Balaclava reaches down and takes Cyril by the arm, and yanks him to his feet. Cyril teeters but manages to hold his footing. "Pops, you better look *real* careful. If I pull this trigger, everything goes. Remember that. Everything. You've got a lot riding on this."

Cyril begins a slow search, opening bedside table drawers, a small desk against the wall, the kitchen drawers. As he searches, he says to Balaclava, "I don't know how we're going to work this if I do find the key. You know a person has to sign in at the bank and show identification to get into a safe box. They're not going to just let you go walking into their vault even if you have a key."

Balaclava thinks about this. He seems so frustrated I fear he is on the verge of just pulling his trigger and commencing the slaughter. But he says, his voice shaking with fury and impatience, "Then you're going to have to make the trip with the key, gramps! Cash will be easier for me anyway. And I'll just stay here with your delightful friend until you come back with the dough. That should make you move fast— thinking about all the dead bodies that are going to be here if you don't get back here quick—especially granny's here. I'm going to do her up real pretty. She's got a smart mouth, and she's already pissed me off."

"How much money are we talking about?" I try to intervene—to divert his cruel talk. I know nothing of Cyril's award.

"Fifty thousand big ones!" Balaclava snaps.

I express true amazement. "That is a *lot* of money!" I am trying to shift emphasis and draw the beast's attention away from his murderous thoughts. Saying that amount out loud seems to calm him for a moment. It reminds him that what he *really* wants is the money, not a lot of dead old bodies.

Cyril is rattling things around in kitchen drawers now. He slams a cabinet door shut, and shuffles back into the room. His head is down, as if expecting still another blow. "I don't think I will find the key here," he admits slowly.

Balaclava is turning the color of a cured ham. He's going to explode. Quickly Cyril says, "But I remember where it is now."

"Where the hell would that be, you fucking mummy? Don't try any more shit with me!"

"The key is in the bookstore in Viroqua. The Brontë sisters have a locked cash box in the back of their store. I gave the key to them for safekeeping when I received the award. I knew if I kept it myself I would forget where I put it. The bookstore is right next door to the bank. It won't take a minute more for me to go into the store tomorrow morning and get that key from them. They open at nine, too."

Balaclava is percolating again, but he manages to control himself. There's too much at stake for him now—and he is beginning to realize this. If he starts shooting everybody, he's only going to end up with dead bodies. He's taken a big chance to come back to Soldiers Grove—and he wants that money in his hands. He is obviously a slow thinker, but he's getting the idea. Cyril is nudging the beast's nasty thoughts around an uneasy corner to this realization. But I am not sure what Cyril is up to with this bank box thing, and it worries me.

"Okay," Balaclava says finally. "No goddamned limousine ride then. *All* of us are going to take a ride to Viroqua in grandma's blue Dodge tomorrow morning. I'll be watching from the truck with her when you go into the store. If I see anything fishy, just the slightest hint of a trick—everything's going to go down. This gun fires probably sixty bullets a minute. I've got two extra clips. I can do a whole lot of damage pretty quick. Half the town should be out on the streets by that time of the morning. I'll take a lot of people with me, and your old lady here is going to go first. Just remember this. I'll *do* it! I don't care, got nothing better to do." He sits down on the edge of the bed again, breathing hard.

"Now, you best get your rest, old folks. It's going be a long night, and there's a lot coming up in the morning besides the sun."

Cyril and I lie down at each end of the long couch. Balaclava stays in the easy chair with his ultimate gun on his lap. Despite our exhaustion we cannot sleep. The night is agony, a few brief, tortured slips into menacing subconscious, only to awaken the next instant trembling. There are no words in the darkness. Balaclava allows us to make only a few necessary trips to the bathroom.

My whole life does not pass before my eyes during these extreme hours, but I think of it in bits and pieces. I came to America from France to a farm in the quietude of the Wisconsin countryside, doing human things, cooking, being a wife, writing, reading, painting, listening and playing music, gardening. Tomorrow in these late hours of my life, there could be sudden, unthinkable violence—and many people, including gentle Cyril and I, might die. This is a lot to ponder in the long mysteries of an aged person's night.

Somehow, suddenly Cyril and I have been propelled to the very core of evil.

CHAPTER 23

Cyril

By the time we reach the outskirts of Viroqua in the blue truck I still haven't thought of what I am going to do when we reach the bookstore.

Of course there is no spare key in the bookstore safe. I made all that up. When I was rummaging around in those drawers in my room, pretending to look for a key—I was really trying to find the sheriff's warning device; but God save my miserable, disappearing mind—I could not find it! Even if I had—what would have happened if the sheriff had suddenly stormed into the room with his gun out, or had the place surrounded with loudspeakers and floodlights. We would all have been killed. Other innocent people would have died. Balaclava has the artillery. He doesn't care.

I made up the business about the bank-box key because I wanted to get the beast out of the home and away from all the residents he was threatening to massacre. I thought maybe I could figure something out before we reached the bookstore in Viroqua, but my head is void as we whisk through the familiar outskirts of town. I feel weak, but now I am going to have to do *something*.

෴

THE PROBLEM of getting the hulking Balaclava out of the rest home early in the morning without being noticed had made me shaky. I was terrified that if he were challenged in some way by the staff, he might go—as they say these days—ballistic, right then. But this did not turn out to be a problem. By arrangement, I went out the front door past the desk, acting as if I were going for a prebreakfast morning walk on the grounds. Then I slipped around to the locked side entrance and held the alarm clapper down as Louise and Balaclava eased out.

Balaclava was goading us along as fast as we could hobble around the building. Just as we turned the corner and started shuffling toward the parking lot, there was the large figure of Danderman standing in the middle of the sidewalk, apparently out for his morning constitutional.

Hosanna! I thought. Big and bad Danderman will now show his mettle. Brute on brute! But when Danderman saw the looming silhouette of Balaclava against the morning sun, he stopped and looked as if he'd gargled Liquid-Plumr. The ex-macho man, without a word or any sign of support for us, fell back and quickly skedaddled away on his crutch, almost going head first in his haste, toward the entrance of the home.

I could see Balaclava consider shooting him down—he even had his big gun out. But if he started blowing people away now, he wouldn't get my money. He was furious. "That son of a bitch might blab his mouth off as soon as he steps inside that building. Come on you corpses! *Move* your asses."

But he couldn't shove us or we would fall down. Instead he jabbed us painfully with the butt of his gun. Louise and I shambled along as best we could to the blue Dodge in the parking lot, and, after we had managed to grope our slow way into the truck, with Balaclava bellowing at us, Louise drove us along the back row of cars out to the highway.

Across the road from the home, Burkum's Tap's sign was dark, and there were no cars gassing up at the Mobil station. It was right there at one of those pumps that this whole thing started.

The day was clear and the sun just slipping above a light ground fog to brighten the tops of the driftless hills around us. The world looked very soft and beautiful. But Louise and I were in a very hard place.

༺ঌ

As we drive into Viroqua I consider trying to tell a few lives to Balaclava—maybe an account of someone's life of historic benevolence. What idiocy! No tale of compassion would ever move this fiend. No story has ever touched his strange, cold mind. He is not a man of stories. He is a man of death, not of lives. He doesn't care. How did he get into *my* life?

But I've got to *do* something. Everything is riding on me.

When I was a lonely kid I read the whole Bible (a premium from the encyclopedia publisher) one summer. I remember an odd passage from Ecclesiastes, something about compassion. I often memorized things as the din of my parents' butchery rose from the rooms below. As Louise drives into town, I recite Ecclesiastes: "For the Lord is full of compassion and mercy, long suffering, and very pitiful, and forgiveth sins, and saveth in time of affliction." At least at this dire moment, this is the best I can do.

Balaclava snarls like an attack dog. "What are you babbling at now, you garbage head? Shut your fucking trap!" He fingers his trigger, and I shut my fucking trap.

But what am I going to do when we get to the bookstore? I think again about the little pistol strapped under my shirt, but there is no way I can fumble it out with my chicken claws before Balaclava blasts me. Louise is pulling the blue Dodge into a parking place across the street from the bookstore now, and I still don't have a plan.

"Move it, geezer!" Balaclava orders, and I pick up my two canes, turn the door handle and swing my skinny legs out. I'm so weakened with fear I almost tumble as my feet touch the pavement, but this is no time for falling down! I gain my bearings and totter my way across the street. My magnificent friend, my Louise, my one and only love, is still back there in the truck with Balaclava, and I am desolate beyond imagination. I will do *something*. Quite what, I don't know yet.

I see through the store window across the street that Emily Brontë has just switched the lights on in the store and is busy turning on her cash register. I mince across the pavement and she looks up as I enter the door.

"Cyril!" she says. "What a nice surprise. What are you doing up so early?"

I'm appalled with myself for having involved the Brontës in this thing. Shame, shame on me! Why hadn't I just given Balaclava the money back at the home? Because, I remind myself, he would have slaughtered us all anyway.

Emily is studying the bruises and cuts on my face. Before she can say something, "Emily," I say. "Something's happening. Don't look out the window now," I say emphatically, "but the beast man has his gun on Louise in the blue truck and he's going to do something very bad if we don't do this right."

Emily instinctively begins to lift her eyes to the window.

"Don't! Emily, for God's sake, *please*, don't look out the window! He's watching. Act like everything is okay. He has the biggest gun in the world out there and he will blow us all away. Please do exactly as I tell you and maybe we can get through this thing. Go into your stockroom for a minute or two and come back out with something very small like a key in your hand. Put it into my hand. Don't ask questions now. He's watching. I *mean* it, Emily. Please, please, please just do as I say."

Emily has had her own moment with Balaclava, she sees my distress and recognizes the peril. She does as I ask, going through the open door into the back stockroom. "What's he going to do?" she calls out from behind the shelves.

"I don't know. But I made up a story about having some money in a bank box, and told him I gave you the key to keep in your store safe for me."

~ 173 ~

"My God! What's he going to do when he finds out it's not here?"

"Emily, I don't know. If I had time to apologize to you I would do so on my knees; but I am going to try and keep things at a minimum and get him away from here before he blows his gourd. You better come out now with a paper clip or something, and put it in my hand. Try to look calm. *Don't* look out the window!"

Emily reappears. As she places the clip in my hand I can feel her tension rise. Of the Brontë sisters, Emily has the bad temper. "This is ridiculous, that man is a menace!" she exclaims. "We cannot just let him intimidate us like this. I'm going to dial 911." She brings up the phone from behind the counter and starts dialing.

"Emily, for God's sake!" But she has already punched in the magical three digit number.

I look out the window across the street. Balaclava has of course seen what is going on and is piling out of the car. He has started to rumble toward us, his monster repeater gun in his paw.

Emily speaks urgently into the phone, "This is the Viroqua bookstore. Send help! We're under attack." She lets the phone dangle and watches the brute come toward us. "My God, look at him!" she says. "The ferocity!" She is remembering his petulant, brutal manner when he came into the store to ask for my whereabouts. Her face is crimson. "He's like an evil alien. Where did he come from? Look at him!"

"Emily, for God's sake, get down!" I urge her, but she skitters back into her stockroom again and comes out with something in her hand, hidden along her arm—not a gun, but a small crowbar which the Brontës must use to open big boxes.

It is absurd. I have never felt so helpless in my life. At that moment I know we are all doomed, and it is my fault.

Do something, fool! I begin tearing my shirt front open and fumbling my own small gun out of its holster, expecting at any moment a blast and shatter of bullets and glass.

Balaclava is close to us in the low rising light. He has been many places, done many awful things. He has his huge gun up. He is pointing with it. He doesn't care. We're finished.

Then with the suddenness of a lightning snap, he is down on the ground, crying out, the big gun skittering out of his hands along the asphalt.

CHAPTER 24

Louise

Whon Balaclava sees Emily take out the phone in the bookstore, he roars with fury and shoves past me out of the truck. I watch him begin to slowly advance across the street toward Cyril and Emily in the bookstore, hunched like a deadly mercenary with his weapon drawn. He is bellowing obscenities.

My God, we are all going to die! I must try to do *something*. I have Heath's pistol out of my handbag, press the pistol against my abdomen and pull the hammer back into place with my arthritic thumb. I almost fall face first onto the pavement as I open the truck door and step out, but gain my footing quickly.

Balaclava is more than halfway across wide Main Street by now. I take a painful step toward him without my cane, stop, spread my legs and reach out to point my gun as Heath taught me years ago. What do I aim at? His head, his back, his legs? He must go down now! Quickly.

I level my sight on the beast. Heath had told me, *hold your breath, and squeeze the trigger slowly.* Balaclava is almost to the bookstore door now as Cyril and Emily cower behind the window. I close one eye, aim at what I hope is the monster's heart, and fire the gun. The recoil knocks me onto my bottom, but I feel no pain except for the sudden ringing in my ears.

Balaclava is writhing on the ground, his weapon fallen from his hands.

CHAPTER 25

Cyril

Balaclava falls on his face and his weapon tumbles from his hands. Has he tripped? Had a heart attack? He's writhing in pain on the pavement. I have my own weapon out now, and find that I can scramble without my two canes; scooting like a hermit crab under a borrowed shell, I am out the door skipping and lurching over to where the monster is down.

When I reach him I see his right shoulder bleeding profusely. Over by the blue Dodge Louise is sitting on the ground with her smoking pistol.

Louise, my darling! My Belle Starr!

But Balaclava is beginning to recover and he's trying to reach out for his weapon. I'm going to have to give him another shot. I raise my gun, but as I do this I hear another noise, an incredible banshee shrieking, and Emily Brontë whooshes past me with her crowbar raised. She rears back and conks Balaclava's head hard—and there is a sound like a punted football. But the beast is still moaning and reaching out, so Emily raises the bar and lets him have it again—right on his coconut. This time he remains still. She gives him still another whack just for good measure.

A few days ago I had read in Louise's new Brontë book, some of the last lines of poetry that Emily Brontë had written just before she died. I know this is an absurd time to think of this—but I am Cyril and, like Popeye, I yam what I am. I am

~ 177 ~

remembering Emily's last lines: "No coward soul is mine, / No trembler in the world's storm-troubled sphere . . ." Emily Brontë had once single-handedly beat the living snot out of a dog handler who had mistreated her animals. I mean, she smacked him around good.

Louise! Emily! My God! The tiger ladies! I am saved. Emily picks up Balaclava's formidable weapon and levels it on him. Louise has staggered over to join us. We are all ringing him now and pointing our weapons down at his bloody carcass— the fearsome Three Furies, a silhouetted triad of senior fury in the rising morning light. If Balaclava awakens and makes another move, he will end up like a Wisconsin swiss cheese dipped in salsa.

It's over. The citizens of Viroqua are gathering warily on the sidewalk to look at this spectacle in wonder. There we are—three white-haired senior citizens with gats in our hands, circling a bleeding body. *No one* has ever seen anything like this before. It must look like a Weegee photograph. No one ventures too close. None of the citizens have the faintest idea what this incredible scene of victory means.

A siren is advancing from the distance through the streets of Viroqua. It is the sheriff. He leaves his red lights blinking when he arrives and his siren on. He hustles out of his cruiser and runs toward us, his brimmed hat tilted forward, his weapon out, his badge glinting. He stoops to check Balaclava's pulse, looks at the wounds in his shoulder and on his head, then stands again to look at the three of us, one at a time, carefully. He lowers his head to his cell phone to call an ambulance, then turns again to us.

"Well, you nailed him pretty good," he says. "You can all put your weapons away now."

"These ladies," I babble at the sheriff, pointing at Louise and Emily. "They *drilled* him!"

"He doesn't look like he's going anywhere," the sheriff agrees.

So it is over. Louise brings the monster down with one shot, and fearless, fearsome Emily finishes him off by creaming him with three ferocious blows to his head, while I stand around with my mouth open. This brute—who'd left me out for dead in a blizzard, who'd clubbed me with a pistol, threatened Louise, insulted Emily, stalked us and threatened us, and tried to steal my money—he's down there bleeding, out cold on the pavement in Viroqua, Wisconsin, dispatched by two elder maidens. I take their hands, both of them—they are weeping with relief, and I join their blubbering. We put our white heads together.

We can hear the approaching ambulance siren. The sheriff stoops again to check Balaclava's head; he looks at the harsh wound in his right shoulder, but slips handcuffs on him—just in case. Then the emergency vehicle arrives and the monster is given a quick bandage and loaded onto a stretcher, tied down, and hauled away mumbling, his shackled hands jammed beneath him. "I'll be along in a minute," the sheriff instructs the ambulance crew.

He turns to look at the three of us again, one at a time. His small moustache twitches over his upper lip. He shakes his head in wonder. "My God!" he says. "You old folks play rough."

CHAPTER 26

Cyril

I do it: I get the money from under my mattress. It has stayed warm in the wool socks. I pay someone to drive me to La Crosse to a travel agent, and lay out serious bucks for two roundtrip first-class airline seats on a passage from Madison to Chicago to Paris, plus wheelchair service and a classy rental car out of Paris. We will be as comfortable as we can be. It doesn't matter that I have no idea what I am doing. I *do* it. And I pay the agent in cash.

It's amazing, the powerful effect a little money can have on you. You sweat as you peel out those bills into other hands, but it is all very exciting, very satisfying. There's a bit of swing in my hobble as I leave the travel office and go to my ride back to the home.

I surprise Louise with the tickets on her birthday. Usually I'm the one who is timorous about our frolics, but now I am the one who has gone all the way, and Louise is the one who gets a little shaky. She is dazzled by the gift. "But aren't we too old for such a trip?" she wonders. "All that money, Cyril! What if one of us gets sick overseas?"

"Then they will have to tend to us," I say. "What are embassies for? We pay taxes for them. They can have us cremated and sent home in urns. To hell with atrophy! Let's go! At our age, we must move until we cannot move."

We arrange a leave of absence from the home. I don't think they've ever done such a thing before. Another first. The staff is unnerved by our plans, never expecting to see us again.

But we have become local legends and made the home famous. The Brontë sisters have become notables, and their bookstore flourishes too, almost a landmark. More eastern reporters travel in from far-flung places to interview all of us and take our pictures. Tourism is up. I remark to one camera about the irony of how we are being honored for the one violent act of our lives—but not for our decades of quiet living. The broadcasters cut this section out.

When we appear on the national newscasts we look so old and tired. Such a strange couple we are—beautiful Louise, and me, with a lopsided head and strawberry nose. People must think we are a couple of cuckoos. Well, so. But Louise and Cyril are going to escape all this folderol! We are going to France! And when we come home we will be nobodies again. There will be other somebodies. But we will have each other.

Louise and I brave the whole plane trip, the chaotic, pre-occupied airports, the shuttles, limousines, and cabs through to Chicago. Our hired wheelchairs get us to the gates, and we endure the soporific seven-hour-long flight, the French car rental, the European traffic circles out of de Gaulle, the salty honking of French drivers.

Brave, incredible Louise is driver and I am navigator. She takes us right into Paris perfectly to our very good hotel in the Marais district. She leaves our car with the parking attendant. Louise! Doing this as if she's been doing it all her life.

The hotel is fairly new and immediately presents us with modern electronic challenges. It takes me a long time to figure out that I have to put our card key into a slot to make the electricity and lights go on. I never do figure out the trendy light system, no matter how many buttons I push. And we also find that the French just *go* to the bathroom, there is no door on it, just an opaque glass wall between the toilet and living area. It is enough to freeze my bowels. But we learn, us old folks, and we get it done. *Vive la France!*

Coming back to the hotel about ten o'clock after a late dinner one evening I am struck that there are almost no older people on the streets. Young people own the nights, couples, singles, gender-disguised or straight, all seeming to be on the prowl. We are the only white-haired people there, and we are not on the prowl. We toddle along.

We take our time in the great city, just stroll and gaze for a few days, nursing our jet lag, Louise using her flawless French to order drinks and meals for us, Louise remembering her visits to Paris as a young woman, when there were no Burger Kings, not a McDonald's or a Starbucks, no people walking about with vacant eyes, speaking into cell phones. "They were all existentialists then," she tells me. "They didn't look at you then either. In Paris one must go within. The city is still here, I can feel it, as it always will be." And so we take to the elegant side streets that she remembers, buy our *glacés* (the most memorable, a dip of black currant for Louise and a *poire* for me), and afternoon aperitifs in the smaller cafés and shops. I remember a light lunch of perfect shaved smoked salmon and goat cheese salad that will stay in my memory the brief rest of my life. We discover couscous and Indian food and Italian beyond spaghetti and meatballs. I even eat snails, and love them.

Then, by God—and each other—after four glowing days in the City of Light, we get in the rental car and Louise takes the wheel again to drive us all the way out into the countryside to begin our journeying, to Lyon, Nice, Toulouse, Carcassonne, Pau, Aix-en-Provence, Puivert, Marseille, Poitiers, and other rare towns large and small, even a dip down into Spain for a brief two days in Barcelona.

In Barcelona I have a moment which tests my aging to the limit: Louise and I are strolling on Las Ramblas, enjoying the shops and open stalls, performers, cafés, mimes, jugglers, and "living statues." Barcelona seems to be a rambunctious, venerable city. Its energy and history are palpable, and young people work at extending the traditions. On these bright days it is like an exotic circus. Louise and I walk as much as we can, then rest on benches, or take slow refreshment in one of the tapas bars.

I am swinging along on my canes past an open flower stall when a street clown, who has been entertaining a tourist crowd, picks up on my weary-looking shuffle as I pass. I glare at him and this prompts him—he begins to follow close at my heels to imitate and mock my staggering gait. Louise has gone ahead to look at some clothing stalls and sees none of this. The clown staggers at my heels and sings a sauntering Spanish song, mimicking my weary steps.

I'll just keep walking, I think. *I'm a stranger here—a guest in this 2,000-year-old, deeply cultured city. I'll ignore this presumptuous fool and maybe he will just go away.*

But he does not go away, keeps tagging along behind and imitating my shuffling gait as I grind along on my canes. He is a clown and perhaps is expected to make fun of everyone, even old men. They snicker nervously as they make way for us.

I do not like being the joke. I feel something damp on the nape of my neck, and turn to see that the fool is dabbing me with shaving cream from a can. Finally he places his silly orange hat on my head from behind to see what I will do as I dotter along.

When he does this, I am so angry and humiliated, I want to turn around and drop the son of a bitch with one of my canes. It is impossible, of course. And even if I do turn on him, he will only skitter away from my fumbling, and make more fun of me. People would think I was a nasty old man.

So I am a "good sport"! It is one of my hardest moments—that I have come to this—to be the stooge. But I waggle my head and arms, pretending to stumble a bit on purpose to look even more like a geezer under the clown's ridiculous hat, becoming the fool myself for the crowd.

At last he lets off, takes his hat back and goes off to mock someone else.

So to escape the clown, I became the clown. My red nose and one floppy ear. My cantilevered walk. The clown's silly hat on my head. Oh, some people loved it, and laughed.

I don't tell Louise about this incident until evening when we are in our hotel room. And I don't tell all—the feeling of vulnerability we are sometimes compelled to feel as elders. It is no time to talk of such things.

Still, Louise is livid—so angry that she weeps. She holds me. We have grown old, but nothing in our lives prepares us for indignities. No choice. We will rest and go on. We hold each other some more. It is but one bad moment.

We drive back up to southern France and into the countryside, the two of us, just taking our good time, staying in very nice hotels with concierges who fuss over us. Louise orders our wonderful meals, buys our patés, soft cheeses and baguettes for our midday meals. And yes, wine for lunch. You bet! Just a small glass.

We travel to Louise's old home area in Surmont—and find it all sadly changed. No trace of her family, no artifacts, no warm nostalgia to cling to, no familiar ghosts nor hints of the past. Her old family house, which the current tenants—after some persuasion and the passage of a few euros—kindly allow us to look in, is completely changed and redone. Only a few phantom memories for Louise: A corner where she sat and read books as a child, another nook that seems familiar, perhaps an original chandelier. I hold her hand as she shuffles through her old home remodeled beyond recognition with new paneling, plastic moldings, three television sets. I know she is very sad that her early French story has been so completely obscured. I expect her to weep, but delicate Louise is made of whipcord.

We move on, and as we travel, I conjure up in my head the many brief and famous lives that have made up the history of France—too many names to name, so many lives to remember. I only occasionally press a few of these on Louise.

But as we drive I read aloud to her from the ceaselessly cheerful guidebooks. Some days we don't go very far at all before we have to stop in a town, take a hotel room, and proceed to an afternoon nap like sensible old folks. After our rest, we rise to stroll in these ancient out-of-the-way places, shopping store windows, then choosing a restaurant for the evening. We eat miraculous regional meals, sip marvelous wines.

At last we return to Paris for our final two weeks. We walk and talk in the great city until we are compelled to rest in cafés. It has been many decades since Louise has been in Paris. Of course it is not the Paris she remembers from her visits as a child. But my Louise—she looks so exquisite and perfectly in place under these trees, she *belongs* in these venerable streets—almost as if she had never left to spend her life near Soldiers Grove.

What does Bogie say to Bergman near the end of *Casablanca?* "We'll always have Paris." I reach often for Louise's hand and hold it.

A great chunk of my "prize for valor" is gone. Who gives a damn? It was all a chimera anyway. I've never felt brave in my life. What a wonderful revel this has been—just the two of us wandering freely in Paris and the beguiling French countryside, doing what we can do.

To just hint at the serendipity of our travel, I'll recall a resonating day we had in the French countryside just before returning to Paris: We were making our way through the northern countryside, driving through a pretty village called Moledor. We stopped for late morning coffee and I noticed a poster advertising a jazz festival in the area going on that very weekend. Moledor seemed to be a lively place with interesting stores and a nice market.

Crowds were coming in for the festival and excitement was mounting. We could hear the opening acts from the square in the distance. Jazz has always excited me, drawn me into its drive and passion. Louise also has great love for this music.

We decided to stay the day in Moledor and treat ourselves. With some effort we found a hotel in a nearby town that could accommodate us for the night. The festival was not a major event, but small and spirited. The groups were all French; some names I remember are Big Band Roquette and Pompon Swing. It was fascinating to hear European musicians swinging the great arrangements of Count Basie and Duke Ellington. There was even a trio that had absorbed the sound of the King Cole Trio, and the pianist sang Nat Cole's tunes, "Sweet Lorraine," "Paper Moon," "I'm Glad There Is You," with a French accent over the guitar and bass.

There was a break in the program, and Louise and I went to have a small beer in a lively café where people were excited about the music. A big Spanish band called Batucada started its set before we finished our beer. We sat and enjoyed their playing as it resounded through the beautiful medieval square. When we returned to the performance area we saw there were eighteen musicians dressed in light band jackets and spiffy panama hats. A lovely girl was on the stand with them, also wearing a hat, and we waited for her to sing.

The musicians were proud performers and their music was Latin, very warm and crafted—the kind of music that demands that you move some part of your body as you listen. Louise and I were swaying together on our canes, and people were beginning to drift out onto the small dance area in front of the band—mostly solitary dancers wishing to express themselves.

There was one very small woman, with a stocking cap pulled down over her gray hair. She was wriggling and hopping. There was something a bit askew about her, not quite right as she moved, but she was enjoying herself immensely as she squirmed around in front of the bandstand.

Some couples started coming onto the floor, several of them really accomplished dancers, flowing and turning, dipping, passing back and forth as they held hands and tossed their heads lightly. Finally there were some older dancers who joined the rest as the music beckoned irresistibly.

Louise poked me gently, looking at me imploringly. What on earth? She was saying something I could barely hear over the music.

I thought she said, dance. She wanted us to do our cane dance right there in the middle of La Belle France. Oh my God, we were such *anciennes*, such Americans! We would look like fools, I thought. They would call the *gendarmes*, call an ambulance, and rush us to *thérapie*. Please, I thought, Louise, no! I shook my head, but she was pulling on my arm.

I had already been made a spectacle in Barcelona; I wanted no more European mockery, but my beautiful friend was guiding me firmly to the floor. I had forgotten to take a pee before we left the café . . . I was in trouble.

"Louise," I pleaded. "I don't remember how to do it." But she kept me moving along toward the dance floor. "You remember very well!" she said. "It was one of your greatest moments. Come on!"

So, there we were standing on a dance floor in France, facing each other—two American basket cases leaning on their canes. Mercy on my mortifying bones! Spare me! The French were stepping back to see what we would do.

Facing each other we dipped to the left, dipped to the right, then slowly turned all the way around several times on our planted canes. More people were gathering around us now. They were cheering. Great God! We faced each other again, tapped our canes together, then tucked them under our arms, embraced and made a half dozen very slow turns in each other's arms to the Latin beat. At last we stopped, let go and stepped back, tapped our canes together again and waved them to the crowd to show we were done.

Had we both become clowns? No, no, no. This was our show, it was what we could *do*, and it was enough. There was a quiet pause—then a large French *tumulte*, delighted clapping and cheers, perhaps even greater than it was at Burkhum's Tap in Soldiers Grove, Wisconsin. We bowed once more to the crowd. We had become troopers. Selective and brief—but *troopers*. The French wanted us to do it again. *Encore!* they cried.

But no, no. We had given all our art.

As we moved off the floor, amidst admiring French chatter, I was feeling the power of what we had done. We moved to the edge of the crowd, and I announced to Louise: "I'm getting into this thing. We're the Cane Dancers. We can really *do* it. Let's practice and put our show on the road in France. *Frédéric and Gingembre*, we can call ourselves. We'll be a sensation! The Elderhoofers. We'll lay them in the aisles in Marseille . . . in Lyon and Toulouse. We're going to need an agent. We need to make more money to take more trips. Italy! England! Tokyo! Moscow! Louise, we'll dance our way around the world!"

Louise was giggling. "I wonder if the bream are biting on the Kickapoo today?" she said as she patted my head to cool me off.

Batucada had grooved into another number, a familiar-sounding, slow tango, and everyone was dancing again. Louise and I were tired, we stepped back away from the movement, trying not to topple over, enjoyed the warm sounds, just moving our bodies slightly as we stood leaning and swaying against each other.

An elderly, very tall, Spanish-looking man, came onto the floor and went to the tiny gray woman with the stocking cap, who had been jumping up and down in front of the bandstand. He took hold of her firmly and suppressed her wriggling, made her focus directly on his face as he talked to her gently. He made her concentrate. He removed her hat, lovingly straightened her gray, tangled hair with his fingers. He took her hand in one of his, and with the other reached down to grasp her waist, and they began to tango, a remarkable high and low movement—pause and hold, swirl and stop—clasped hands holding and releasing as he reached down to dip her, turning beautifully, flowing and proud, the two of them, the man content, the woman transformed, amazing together and so opposite.

The man looked far out into the distance over her uncombed hair as they danced. I imagined he might be remembering things from his past—challenges, losses, disappointments, triumphs—looking back because he was old and had little in front of him now, perhaps recalling times when he was too young to even imagine death; perhaps moments of bravery and love long gone, but remembered quietly in this dance with the small woman on an outdoor ballroom floor in France where so many of us were far from our homes and almost finished with our lives.

CHAPTER 27

Louise

We have been back from France and in the home for some time now. Both of us have gotten very sick; then both of us got well again. We take many medicines, our pill boxes spill over. At times we feel strange, a mysterious medicinal, aged drifting, a vagueness which we do not welcome.

There is no need to describe in detail our final exhaustion. Eventually everyone comes to it, this permanent malaise, this denouement one cannot predict or cure when it finally appears. It is always out there, ready to swoop in on us in its time, and when it arrives, it is manifest.

Each part of us seems to be paying up at once: teeth, eyes, legs, ears, arms, mind, heart, spleen, stomach, and intestines go afoul, and lungs, bowels, hair, feet, fingers, tongue. Here is our dust, the age which makes us all smell like diapers and soiled washcloths, which sometimes causes us to slip and fall down like shabby overcoats from closet hangers and lay stunned in crumpled heaps.

It would be easy enough to constantly complain about these final events, but Cyril and I do not feel cheated. Somehow we were also given a charmed finale when we no longer thought such things were possible, experiencing more in the last year together than through all our previous years. It was like a thrilling short novel—mysteries, discovery, romance, adventure, challenge, fear, threat, chase, violence, triumph, travel, love, tenderness, devotion.

Above all, now we have memories of our endearment. Each night in Paris in the weeks before the end of our great trip, Cyril came into my bed and we had our quiet, happy love again, unclothed in the night of the City of Light, together just touching and holding each other until we slept.

I cannot imagine through what impossible mix of human existence these moments were given to us at our conclusion—and yet this bandaged man who knows all the lives, near the last moment for both of us, had sat down beside me in the Soldiers Grove Care Home dining hall and asked me if I had ever heard of Christine de Pisan.

And I had! By the grace of whichever or whatever God you wish to believe in, I *had* known who that obscure medieval woman was; so Cyril and I were given each other for this last bit of time together.

One evening, as he embraced me and I cradled him with my hand, a secretion, a small passage of love, came and completed his life, making him writhe with pleasure. Cyril tossed his battered head back, loudly rejoicing, waving his claws like a snowbird on the sheets, his strawberry nose bright in the soft glow of Paris streetlamps.

I was so happy for him. All his words, all those years— and now this punctuation.

After this happened, Cyril clung to me as if I were about to disappear. Yes, of course, I am about to disappear. But even approaching this final mystery—doesn't one weep with joy on such occasions? At least we did. Cyril and I, we did, and we do.

·